WHEN SHE'S PREGNANT

A RISDAVERSE NOVELLA

RUBY DIXON

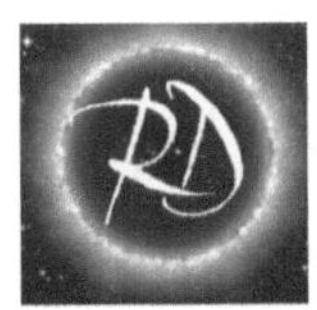

For all the bitches that like a baby book

(It's me, I'm bitches)

WHEN SHE'S PREGNANT

Naomi has spent her entire profits from her farm's yield for a fertility shot. She wants a baby to ease some of the loneliness of life at the edge of the universe. Unfortunately for her, the donor she had lined up can't finish the job. What's a lonely, ovulating human to do?

This one heads to the Port Custodial office and asks for help from the military custodian on duty.

Brawny but awkward Ainar isn't sure why this human is insisting on needing his help for *sleeping*, but he's happy to assist someone as delicate and pretty as the human colonist. And when he figures out what she really wants...well.

Surely this is a dream come true.

This novella is stand-alone, high-heat and low-angst, which means it's pretty much awesome. You do not have to read other Risdaverse novellas in order to read this one (though characters from other stories will drop in).

CONTENT NOTE

In an effort to be mindful of triggers for readers, I've included the following list. If I've missed something, please write me and let me know.

Please skip if you are avoiding spoilers!

SPOILERS BELOW SPOILERS BELOW SPOILERS BELOW SPOILERS BELOW SPOILERS BELOW SPOILERS BELOW SPOILERS BELOW SPOILERS BELOW SPOILERS BELOW

This particular story has (in no particular order):
- Abandonment themes
- Infertility theme
- Pregnancy plot
- Class/Caste issues for the hero
- References of an abusive past for the heroine
- Voyeurism
- Tattoos and piercings (some people don't like them!)

ONE

NAOMI

They're going to think I'm an idiot.

I take a deep breath as I stand outside the Port Custodial Office, biting my lip and worrying. I could turn around and go home. Retreat back to my farm and pretend none of this ever happened. Count the credits as a loss and the rest of it as a lesson learned.

But...then I'll be out my credits and I still won't have a baby. I'll be alone as ever—maybe even moreso because if I lose all these credits, it'll be a long, long time (if ever) I can make them again.

That decides me. With a steeling breath, I grit my teeth and then step inside the office.

Or I try to. I've forgotten that the doors do a quick check-over to identify you, and I run into the glass door, leaving a mark on the pristine surface. The smack I make as I run into it is loud, and I glance around to see if anyone else has seen my humiliating moment. Thank goodness, the street is fairly empty this early in the morning.

The doors fall open, parting like one of the old grocery stores back home, and I step inside. "Welcome to the Port Custodial Office, Colonist Flannigan," the computer chirps helpfully. "Someone will be by to assist you shortly."

"Thank you," I say politely. Part of me wants to run with embarrassment, but a bigger part of me wants the baby I've been promised, so I stay.

The custodian office is rather bland and boring-looking. There's a waiting area at the front with some benches that look a bit too tall for short human legs, and a couple of tables. In the back, I see the "office" itself behind a decorative half-partition that's covered with plas-film flyers of local events—library club, knitting club, first-time farmers meet and greet, missing meat-stock notices, and postings for small jobs. It's an identical board to the one in the courthouse across town, and the sight of it makes me flinch with how innocent I was a few weeks ago when I posted my own notice.

Now I'm just another human female that's been conned out of her credits.

I lower my hood and sit at one of the tables at the front, waiting for someone to come assist me. A lot of things in Port have changed in the last few years, especially since the Port Custodians have arrived. There are fewer mercenaries looking to steal someone or their farm. The guy running the general store no longer charges humans three times as much as everyone else. The people running town are no longer as crooked as they used to be, and it feels safe to be here (even if I do still wear a hood and cloak just to be on the safe side) and I don't have to worry that a praxiian or a szzt is going to accost me if they see my very human head of hair.

Some people aren't fans of the Port Custodians. They're all

mesakkah and military, which means they don't answer to Lord va'Rin directly. They tend to interfere with the black market here, and I know some of the women complain that traders no longer bring Earth contraband to sell to us at a mark-up. That means fewer books, fewer shoes made for humans, fewer... everything. I'll take it, though. I just want to be safe.

Safe...and not lonely.

"Colonist Flannigan is waiting for assistance," the computer calls out helpfully overhead after a few minutes pass.

A male with shiny horns and deep blue skin peers around the corner. He looks younger than the other custodians I've met here, and his gaze flicks around the room before landing on me. "Flannigan?"

"I'm Naomi," I clarify. It feels strange to hear my last name again. I get to my feet. "Is this a bad time?"

"Oh, uh, of course not." He steps forward, a data pad in his hand, and his tail flicks back and forth in what seems like agitation. "I must be the only one on duty. If you want to come back tomorrow, I'm sure Khex or Rektar would be happy to assist—"

"You can't help me?" I ask. "I need help today. Tonight, actually."

"Tonight," he echoes, and then taps his data pad, activating it. "Very well. I'm the only one on duty at the moment, so I will do what I can. Is there a problem with your farm? How would you categorize your distress?"

My...distress? I tilt my head, studying him. I've seen him around Port, but I don't think I've ever spoken to him. There are two military guys that are in charge of everything. Khex is the friendliest and knows everyone. And of course I know Rektar because he's my friend Lucy's quiet, thoughtful husband. From gatherings and local gossip, I know the other Port Custodians are younger and came to this particular outpost because they're considered lower caste in some way. Like they have the wrong family names and therefore they won't get anywhere with their military careers. In a way, this universe has kind of screwed them over, too. I get that.

The male in front of me is a mixture of youthful eagerness and responsible adult. He looks like he could be my age—thirty-two—or maybe older. There's an innocence to his gaze that makes him seem boyish, though. Or maybe it's his long lashes and the curve of his mouth that hasn't hardened into a permanent frown I see on so many world-weary types. I continue eyeing him. He's wearing the smooth gray uniform of the Port Custodians, with the collar done up to his neck. It looks chokingly tight but he doesn't tug on it, and peeking out from the collar are what look like tattoos. He has no piercings that I can see, not even on his ears, and his capped horns look to be plain and without the ornate styling I saw on Lord va'Rin's fancy horns.

He taps a few more things into the pad and then turns his head, checking something in the office behind him, and I notice his neck is rather thick and corded. His arms are, too, now that I peer a little more, like the absolute creeper I am. His uniform is definitely tight across the biceps, and I'm a sucker for nice arms.

"Colonist? Is everything all right?"

I snap to attention, blinking at him. "Hmm?"

"Is something wrong with my appearance?" He gives me a puzzled look. "You were staring at me."

Ooof, busted. "Um...sorry. I'm just, well...I forgot what you asked me."

"How would you categorize your distress?" he asks again, poised to type on his data pad the moment I answer.

Instead, I stare at his hands. Gosh, they're nice hands. His nails are blunted, his fingers long and yet somehow meaty. Boy, I must really be pumped full of hormones if I'm noticing a stranger's hands. He's still waiting for an answer, I realize, and I look up.

I should tell him I've been hoodwinked. Tricked. That someone laid a trap and I fell for it.

I should tell him I need someone to make a baby with me, stat.

Instead, what comes out is, "I need to get laid."

TWO

AINAR

The big problems always show up when I'm at the Custodial office alone. It doesn't matter if Rektar or Khex take only one day off during the month—inevitably on that day, something will happen and anxious human females will flood into the office looking for assistance. Normally Sinath takes charge of things. He gets less flustered around the pretty females. Says he grew up with sisters and he just thinks of them all as his sisters. I think he's a liar, but as long as he handles things, I can busy myself with paperwork instead of having to actually talk to the humans. The newest recruit, a young soldier named Paxon, is out doing his rounds, which means I'm the only one here.

So of course she shows up.

Colonist Flannigan is beyond pretty. She's delicate like all humans are, with dark eyes and dark hair. She has a bump on her nose which I find strangely adorable, and when she smiles at me her teeth are small and white and even. Her voice is sweet and gentle, and she seems distracted enough that she doesn't notice how flustered I am in talking to her.

Ainar vo'Lon has a terrible history with romance. When I first got here, I was besotted with a female colonist who made it clear she was interested in me. I wooed her—probably a bit too rapidly, according to Khex—and offered to mate her. She refused me. But then she kept showing up in Port, and so I'd offer again, only to get turned down once more.

It was only after Khex took me aside and pointed out that human females think differently than we do that I realized I was scaring her instead of wooing her. Back on Homeworld, if you lose your heart to a female, you want to mate her and take care of her forever. I didn't grasp what he meant by females just wanting a "good time" or to "flirt." That constantly asking a female to mate you comes across as 'stalking' and not enthusiasm.

It's just...back on Homeworld, the vo'Lon family is dirt. Worse than dirt. We're garbage collectors and prison spawn and our family name is worthless. No female worth anything would ever look at me, and I've always known that I'm nothing in the eyes of a mesakkah female. Coming here and being surrounded by pretty humans that wanted to talk to me? That didn't care that my family name was trash?

It felt like the answer to every dream I'd ever had.

But my eagerness scared away the female I wanted. It was a painful lesson, made all the more painful when I saw the object of my affections flirting with someone new a few months later. The answer to me was obvious—I come on too strong. Human females don't want a male that is utterly devoted from the first breath. They apparently want to be chased.

I am terrible at chasing. So I do menial tasks in the office. I go on patrol. And I let the others handle the females that come in for assistance.

The human in front of me—Colonist Flannigan—reminds me that my heart is far too eager. She watches me with soft eyes, her gaze moving over my chest and then focusing on my hands.

"How would you categorize your distress?" I gently prompt. I need to follow the criteria and just get her out the door. Handle things quickly so I can't get myself in trouble. Get her out the door so I don't lose my heart.

"I need to get laid," she blurts out.

"Laid where?" I ask, entering this in the data pad. *Colonist is fatigued and requires sleep. Needs to lay down.*

She looks startled at my question. "Uh, I didn't give it a lot of thought? I mean, if you want to help me, I'm totally game for here." She gestures. "The back of your office. On your desk. Wherever."

"Of course I will help you," I say. "It is my duty as a custodian."

She blinks at me. And blinks a bit more. "Um...you're sure about that?" The human raises a hand in the air and gives a little laugh. "Not that I mind, of course. I just thought it would take a little more convincing than that."

"If you want to sleep, of course I can help you." Though I'm not certain as to why she needs my assistance, but she's so lovely and relieved that I am helping her that I feel obligated to assist in any way I can.

"Sleep *together*," she corrects.

That makes me pause. "You need a companion to help you slumber?"

The pretty human—Colonist Flannigan—wrinkles her brows and gives me an odd look. "I'm not talking about *sleeping*-sleeping. I'm talking about fucking."

My tongue sticks to the roof of my mouth. I stare at the female, at her lovely dark eyes and dark hair, and the intense look upon her face. She's anxious and frustrated and here because...she needs male companionship?

From *me*? A low caste mesakkah with a dead-end military outpost job?

I manage to clear my throat. "Apologies, but I think I missed something, colonist."

She winces. "No, I'm sorry. It's my fault. I'm just all over the place. Hormones, you know." A moment later, she leans forward, her face buried in her hands as if she's hiding it from me. "Ugh, this is so embarrassing."

"There is nothing to be embarrassed of. You need assistance, and I am trying to help. That is my duty to the colonists here." It takes all of my willpower to keep my tail from flicking in frantic agitation. I just know that if this female leaves—if I can't be the hero she needs—I'll never forgive myself. I pause and then add a bit more, desperate. "*Please* let me help."

The female straightens, flipping her hair back and squaring her shoulders. She nods and gives me a half-smile. "You're right. You're right. Okay. Let's start this over, shall we?" She sticks her hand out to me. "I'm Naomi Flannigan. I farm plot 4201, out to the east."

I memorize her words as if they are priceless, and clasp her hand in mine. "I am Custodian Ainar." My face gets hot even as I deliberately leave off my shameful family name. I do not want her to think less of me. I continue to grip her hand, and as I do, I feel her tiny extra finger—the strange fifth one all humans have—brush against my palm. It is not as strange as I thought it would be.

This is the first time I am touching a human's hand, I realize. Most come from difficult backgrounds and do not want attention from us at all, or are respectful of hygiene laws. They tend to nod in greeting or simply announce themselves.

I decide I like touching, but only when it comes to Naomi Flannigan. My face gets even hotter, and I imagine what Khex and Sinath will say when they check the feeds in the morning. Oh, how they will laugh at me. I do not care, though. The only thing I care about is that Naomi Flannigan keeps smiling at me.

She smiles sweetly at me and then extricates her hand from my grasp. "Nice to meet you, Ainar."

"I am full of pleasure right now," I confess, my heart beating wildly. I now realize what the others say when they claim that a mesakkah knows his mate instantly and wants to protect her at all costs the moment he sees her. I feel like that right now when I gaze upon Colonist Flannigan—Naomi. I would do anything she asks. This feeling is far more intense than any infatuation I have felt in the past. Is it because I have touched her hand? Or is there something more to our interaction? Something inexpressible?

"You look a little distracted."

"Still full of pleasure," I admit, my face even hotter. But she smiles at me, and I find I am eagerly grinning back at her like a lovesick fool. I want nothing more than to clasp her hand again.

"Well, your day is about to either go downhill or through the roof, depending on how you handle this next part." She takes a deep breath, then continues. "So I had a really good spring crop and was finally able to save up enough money to have a baby."

Ah. I have heard of such things before. Did my co-worker Rektar not go through something similar recently when his Lucy wanted to have a child? They used up all of their savings to work with a fertility doctor who specializes in humans.

"Before you ask, no, I don't have a mate. I'm just kind of tired of the same old thing and spending every day out on the farm alone, it can get lonely. I've always wanted a baby. Several, actually. I didn't think it'd be possible considering alien biology and me being human." She gestures at herself. "And I don't see a lot of human men here. So I figured I was looking forward to a very quiet future. But then my friend Kerri said that there was a doctor who came to Port and helped humans out. That it was how Milly kept getting pregnant."

Lady va'Rin, the lord's wife. She's currently pregnant with her third, I believe. Something tells me she is not using the same physician as the rest of the colonists, but I do not point this out. I wait for her to state why she is here seeking my help. Has this physician defrauded her, perhaps? Or has another colonist stolen some equipment she needs to ensure her pregnancy? I wait patiently, absorbing the details of her appearance, of her lovely skin that is the perfect shade of one of Lucy's strange cookies, that her eyes are framed with long lashes. That the tip of her nose flexes when she smiles.

Naomi, I think dreamily. Her name is Naomi. It is a sound as lovely and pleasing as she is.

"My friend got me in with the doctor, and I brought my savings. He gave me a shot of fertility drugs and another shot of vitamins to help things take, and told me I had a week to get pregnant. I thought I'd just get artificially inseminated, you know? But apparently your people's sperm count drops severely the moment the sperm leaves the body, so I figured heck, I'll do it the old-fashioned way. Get a little drunk, have a little fun, call it a day. I met a guy—"

My stomach lurches unpleasantly. Is she going to tell me all about how this male got her pregnant? Or didn't? Why do I want to punch things at the thought of another mesakkah touching her? I no longer want to hear this story...but she needs my help. It is my duty above all else. So I brace myself. "This male harmed you?"

"No! That's the thing." Her expression is a mixture of laughter and annoyance. "He put me off for a few days, and when I finally cornered him, he confessed that he'd fallen in love with another girl that he was helping get pregnant right before me, and so he couldn't help me get pregnant after all."

I laugh.

Naomi pauses and blinks at me. "Oh. Um."

Oh no. My relief at the fact that this male did not touch her has bubbled over. "Apologies," I blurt out. "I am glad that the trouble with the male is not of a darker nature. That is all."

"Oh. Yeah. I guess I can see that." She gives me a wry smile and the dimple comes out. "There's not a lot of people here with happy stories, are there?"

"Lucy has a good story," I immediately offer.

"Okay, then *one* person does," she manages, and I realize hers must not be a happy story. My stomach curdles slightly at the realization, and I want to grab her and hide her away inside my office, where no one can ever touch her again.

Instead, all I do is clutch my data pad a little tighter. "I see."

I see I will have to figure out an outlet for my rage once she is gone. Perhaps sparring with Paxon. I rather enjoy thrashing him.

We're both silent for a long, uncomfortable moment. "Anyhow," Naomi finally blurts. "I tried to line someone else up to help me out with my situation. Someone that doesn't have any genetic abnormalities and doesn't mind banging a human. Someone that I'm relatively confident won't cut my throat and rob me." She gives me a tight smile. "Doesn't leave me many choices, which is why I'm here."

Disappointment crashes over me. "I see. You require my assistance in finding another male that can impregnate you?" I should be flattered that she trusts the custodians enough to do such a thing. It's a sign of our growing influence among the colonists, who used to be utterly terrified of all law enforcement. I should be happy at this sign, and instead I find myself vaguely wishing Paxon was here so I can murder him in the training room. "I will do my best."

Naomi licks her lips. "Here's the thing."

I find myself staring at her mouth, full and lush. Humans aren't much for sanitary laws, I remember vaguely, and I find I cannot stop staring at her wet, dusky lips. "Y-yes?"

"I'm fertile right now," she says bluntly. "My window is closing very quickly. And...and you seem nice." She sits on the edge of her seat, her hands twisting in her lap. "Please tell me you're not mated? I heard only Rektar and Khex are."

"You came here looking for a custodian to service you?" The words are hoarse. My mind is filling up with all kinds of filthy fantasies. Oh kef, the worst, best kinds of fantasies. Fantasies of bending her over my desk, fantasies of her wet mouth, fantasies of pushing into her while she clings to me, her legs wrapped around my waist—

"What? Oh, oh no!" She laughs, waving her hands. "It's just, um, I was hoping you guys would know someone. And now I'm here and you're nice, and you're cute, and like, I know you won't murder me." Naomi shifts her weight in her chair. "And I'm really, really ovulating and it's affecting me."

"You truly want *me*?" I'm flabbergasted, even as the fantasies start playing through my head again. Will she be dusky and wet between her thighs like her lips, or...

Naomi gives me another little smile and moves closer, her knees bumping mine. "If I don't find someone to make me pregnant in the next twenty-four hours or so, I'm going to lose my savings. Then I'll have no baby and no money. So, unless you've got somewhere else to be and you're not totally averse to the idea, I would love for you to make me pregnant." She pauses, then adds, "Please. It wouldn't be a commitment, either. You don't have to be in the baby's life. I don't intend on raising this child with someone. I just need your sperm, basically."

This is every fantasy I have ever had come to life. For a moment, I think Sinath is pranking me. That he has somehow set this up, knowing I have never touched a female, and even now is somewhere, laughing at me silently. But the desperate look in Naomi's eyes sells this. She is telling the truth.

She truly wants me to impregnate her.

Right now.

I clear my throat. Even though I hate the thought of anyone else touching this glorious creature, I feel I must give her options. "Once again, I must ask if you are certain you want me. Both Sinath and Paxon can be contacted. Both of them are of slightly higher caste than I am."

"Are you telling me no?"

"No! I mean, no, I am saying yes." I run a hand down my face. "I am saying I wish to impregnate you—" Kef, this is getting worse the more I speak. "I just wished to provide you with options. That is all. I am not exactly any female's dream."

She bites her lip, giving me a worried look. "Genetics?"

"What?"

"Are your genetics good? No illnesses that can be passed on to the child?" When I shake my head, she continues. "Are you mated to someone? Attached?"

"No. I am not."

"Great," she says enthusiastically, and then cringes. "I mean, I'm not celebrating that you're alone. I'm just...these shots really have me messed up. You seem nice, and you're cute, and like...I would really like to do something with you." The look she gives me is desperate. "I promise we can be quick.

You don't even have to come inside me if you find humans repulsive. You can jizz in a cup and we can baste it up into the right spot with a utensil or something—"

"I would like to touch you," I blurt out before she can continue. "I would like that very much."

Naomi squirms in her seat. "Oh, thank god. Because these shots are no joke. I have never been so damn horny." Her eyes are a little glassy as she moves forward onto the edge of her seat. "Can we go to your desk or something?"

"Here? Now?"

"I would prefer not to waste any time." She taps her wrist. "Tick tick."

This has to be a joke of some kind, because no female will come in and demand to be serviced, especially not from a male like me. This sounds like Sinath's work. He would tease me in such a manner, but I do not see him. I do, however, smell the distinct perfume of arousal coming off of the human.

That part surely cannot be a joke.

I do not believe in the old gods, but tonight I will be saying prayers to whoever is listening. Because this is a dream, and I do not want to awaken.

"Your desk?" Naomi prompts, her cheeks flushed.

"Yes!" I jump to my feet, hoping she does not notice my already-rigid cock straining the front of my trou. "Please, follow me."

CHAPTER

THREE

NAOMI

I am the sluttiest slut that ever slutted...and I don't even care. Am I about to bone a perfect stranger on his desk at work so he can impregnate me? Absofuckinglutely. Am I excited about this? Ridiculously so. Am I absolutely horny and possessing some extremely damp panties right now? Yes and yes.

When they'd mentioned the fertility shots packed quite a punch, I didn't realize that they would make me want to crawl the walls with the need to be laid. I've been masturbating furiously for the last several days, waiting for my "turn." Now that everything's falling to pieces, I might as well fuck a stranger.

And honestly? This stranger seems nice. Sweet. Kind.

Nervous as hell, too. That's a good sign as far as I'm concerned. That means he'll come quickly, and if I'm lucky, he'll come more than once. I'm quite happy to play the odds, given that I'm low on time. I can practically feel my biological

16

clock tick-tick-ticking away as if it's being broadcast to the entire planet.

I'd be a little embarrassed if I wasn't so horny. As it is, I just want to get laid and get pregnant. I don't want to have suffered with intense arousal all week and spent all my hard-earned savings only to end up with empty arms at the end of this. If it means sleeping with a stranger? I'll sleep with a stranger.

I've had shitty sex plenty of times since I was taken from Earth. What's one more round, after all?

So I give this guy—Ainar—an encouraging look. Unless he wants to fuck right here (and honestly, with every moment that passes, I'm starting to consider it) we need to move to his office. "Your desk?"

"Yes! Please follow me." He jumps up, all eagerness, and I'm reminded of a schoolboy about to get his dick wet for the first time. There's something innocent about his eyes—which is ironic, because the rest of him could put a wrestler to shame. He's got big thick arms and legs, and a broad face with wide eyes. His hair is cut short and the uniform he wears looks neat and tidy. He seems like a good guy. He seems like a two-pump chump, if I'm being honest, but nice.

I could do worse. I could do a lot worse.

When we head to the back of the office, though, I'm a little dismayed to realize that his desk is out in the open with all the others. There's no private office around here, no door to shut and give us some whisper of privacy. His desk is right across from several other desks, and while I'm relieved that he moves towards the one that's neat and tidy, I'm starting to rethink this whole "sex right now" scenario.

It's as if he can read my mind. Ainar turns to me, a look of hesitation on his face. "You are certain? You want to do this right now?"

I'm not so certain, no. But then something inside me

twinges and aches deep inside, like my body is getting ready to bust out with my period, and it makes me panicky. If I want a baby—a reason to wake up every morning—I need to do this ASAP. "This your desk?" I ask, pointing at the one he stands near, his tail twitching. When he nods, I hop up on the edge of it and give him an encouraging look.

Do the blue aliens blush, I wonder? Because Ainar's tail sways back and forth quickly, as if he's trying to contain himself—and losing the battle. "How...ahem, how would you like to proceed?" He clears his throat, and there's a squeak in his otherwise deep timbre. It's kinda cute.

"I wore a skirt," I say helpfully, spreading my legs and feeling absolutely wanton. "You can pull my panties off and then, you know..."

"Ah." He rubs the base of one horn. "Yes. Of course." That tail twitches so hard I'm surprised it's not starting a whirlwind behind him. "Panties."

"Female undergarments?" When he gives a quick nod and still doesn't reach for me, I decide I need to help things along. I lift one butt cheek, tilting to the side, and slip my panties off one cheek and then the other. I shimmy them down my legs and then kick them off my sensible shoes, leaving them on the floor. "Now I'm officially open for business."

Please don't change your mind. Please don't change your mind.

"I should have done that for you," he murmurs, taking a slow step forward. His hand hesitates just above my knee, and when he finally rests it there, I want to groan with relief. "My apologies, colonist. I'm not used to such situations—"

"Naomi," I breathe. "If we're going to do this, you could at least call me Naomi."

"Naomi," he echoes, and it sounds really good coming from him. He gazes down at my parted thighs even as he steps between them, making my skirt slip up to my knees. "May... may I touch you? Just to get the feel for things?"

"Of course." Did I pick the only virgin for miles around? Just my luck. Every other alien I've met would have had me bent over the desk and impaled before I could complete a sentence. This one is being frustratingly, infuriatingly polite.

Sweet, but not what I need right now.

He works one big blue hand under my skirt, and I catch a brief glimpse of tattoos on his palm before it disappears under the fabric. In the next moment, warm fingers skim up my thigh.

I spread them wider, whimpering. Oh god, I really am out of my mind with need right now. It's like an itch that's so close to being scratched. I've never felt like this when ovulating before, but I've also never been hopped up on alien meds, so there's that. "Please go higher," I manage tightly. "I will love you forever if you just go higher."

Ainar gives me a startled look, and then his hand gently brushes over the mound of my sex. The moment he touches me, my body makes a wet, obscene sound. I'm part horrified, mostly aroused, and worried he's going to freak out. Aliens are big into hygiene, and sex is just about one of the messiest things a body can do.

But Ainar doesn't seem to mind. He groans, his fingers dipping into my folds and exploring that silky wetness. He rubs me, moving deeper until his blunt fingertips press up against the entrance to my body. It feels so much like relief that I want to scream.

Then he pulls away, and I want to murder him for not fingering me into an immediate orgasm.

"Ah," is all he says. "I think I have it now."

"Great," I manage, and it takes everything I have not to wrap my legs around him and beg for him to just pound me into the table. I need this so badly. I'm not even thinking about a baby at the moment. I just need—desperately—for someone to touch me and ease this terrible ache. "If you've changed your mind..."

"No. Not at all. If you're sure you want me—"

I grab him by the front of his tunic, pulling him forward, and give him a crazed stare. "If you don't fuck me in the next five minutes, I am going to lose my mind, Ainar."

His eyes widen.

"Sorry. I just...I don't have time to waste." I swear if he turns me down, I'm going to burst into tears. Big, ugly, noisy tears...and that's going to make it hard for me to find someone else. "Like I said, you don't have to even touch me. I just need your jizz—"

Ainar's big hand suddenly covers my chin. He squeezes my cheeks, making my mouth pucker. Then, he leans in and presses his mouth to mine. "Do we kiss first?" He gives me a very studious look as he studies my puckered mouth. "I'm not sure if mine fits on yours properly."

Well, it won't if he keeps squeezing mine like that. "We can kiss some other time," I say quickly. "It's not required for impregnating me."

"Oh, of course not." He looks disappointed.

I fight back a wave of guilt, because I'm literally just asking this guy to fuck me, not to woo me. But I'm down to compromise. "Come first? Kiss later?"

He nods, his hands going to his pants—the thick leggings that the mesakkah wear under a tunic that they call "trou." *Yes.* I'm practically licking my lips at the sight of the bulge that's revealed when he lifts his tunic hem.

"Oh wow," I breathe. "You're, uh, a big boy."

Ainar freezes, his tail stopping mid-swing. "This...is bad?"

Shit. Am I talking him out of things? I shake my head quickly and put my hands over his, fumbling with the strange activated fastener that aliens use on their clothes. "No. It's perfect. I'm just surprised. The last dick I saw was, well, not that big. Or pleasant. But it was long. Not fat. Just long. Fat's better, you know? I mean, not that I'm doing this because I really wanted some fat dick. I just wanted a baby. But dick is a side benefit." He remains paralyzed and when I look up, his expression is stricken. "You know what? I'm going to quit talking about dick now."

"I hope you find mine pleasant," Ainar says, and then unzips.

I swear to god, it's like a snake falls out of his pants. I stare in shock as the biggest, prettiest blue dick reveals itself to me. The head is ever-so-slightly mushroomed at the tip, and a deeper, more velvety shade of blue there. Thick, flaring ridges move up his shaft, and the man has piercings like a compass, with dual metal spider-bites to the north, south, east and west. He's got a curve ever so slightly to one side, and at the base of his shaft is a small cartilage protrusion that I've heard about but have never experienced.

"Oh. Um. Okay," I say quickly. "You should know I've never had sex with a mesakkah. Is there anything I need to be aware of before we proceed?" I glance up at him, and then I can't resist putting my hand on his shaft and stroking it. Oh god, he feels like velvet. I'm torn between demanding that he shove it inside me and petting him like a stuffed animal. "You can't lose a piercing or anything, can you?"

He remains stationary, holding his tunic out of the way so I can admire his impressive cock. I stroke him again and his breath catches, the only outward sign that he's aware of my touch. His eyes are tightly closed.

"Ainar?" I ask when he doesn't respond.

"Take what you need," he manages, his expression one of pure martyrdom. "I am here for you."

Participation. That's what I need. "Sorry. I got distracted. You have a nice cock, though. Good job." I give him an awkward smile. "Feel free to put it inside me at any time."

He lets out a deep breath and his gaze roams over me. "You are still certain you want me?"

"Oh yes," I sigh. "Now that I've taken her for a test drive? Yes please." I resist the urge to touch his dick again—it really, really is a nice dick—and lean back in what I hope is an inviting and baby-making manner. I rest my weight on my hands, and I'm pretty sure I've got my palm on something electronic, but I'm also pretty sure that Ainar hasn't noticed. His gaze is locked on my spread legs and the skirt hiked up between them.

Ainar glances up at my face and then takes a step forward, his thighs hitting mine. Everything inside me clenches in anticipation, and I watch as he takes himself in hand and guides his erection toward the spread of my thighs. *Please*, I pant. *Please please please please.*

When the head of his cock grazes my folds, I practically sob with need. "Yes," I breathe. "Give me a baby. I need this so badly."

He groans, pressing forward. I lift my hips slightly, trying to help, and he slips the head of his cock against the entrance to my body. He's bigger than I expected, and that's the last thought that crosses my mind before he pushes forward, and then he's inside me.

We both gasp at the same time.

As if he can't control himself, Ainar thrusts deeper, seating himself fully inside me. It's been a long time since I've had sex, and longer still since I've been completely stretched by a lover, and the tense fullness of it takes my breath away. My lips part and a wordless sound escapes me.

"Should I stop?" he asks, his voice strained. "Tell me what you need."

"Move," I manage thickly. "Move. Hard. Make me come."

I don't expect him to make me come. Not really. But I've learned that men tend to pop off like rockets when they think they're an absolute stallion in bed, so it's habit to throw something like that out there. Ainar pulls back and surges forward again, the movement graceless and just this side of unpleasant, but he's so thick and I'm so wet and aroused that it's doing exciting things to my body despite his lack of prowess. He starts moving quickly, his hips stuttering against mine, and it pushes that strange protuberance—the spur—against my clit in a rather nice, ticklish sensation.

But then Ainar's breath explodes in a gust and he shudders, and I realize he's come already.

Perfect. I beam at him. "That was amazing. Thank you."

"You..." He pauses, his tail swishing. "That was good for you?"

He looks openly skeptical, as if he's doubting my mental ability to get off from that, and I have to swallow a chuckle. "It felt nice," I admit. "But you came inside me, and that's what I wanted." I press a finger close to where our bodies are joined, and sure enough, there's a ton of thick, viscous fluid there. "Let me know before you pull out. I want to tilt my hips up so I don't lose anything."

"I...very well."

I let out a tiny yelp as he hauls our joined bodies up and then he moves out of me. In the next moment, my bare ass is in the air, my legs hooked over his shoulders.

"How long will you need to stay like this?" Ainar asks me, his voice oh-so-polite and earnest.

I want to giggle at the absurdity of the day. I strolled in off the street, begged a stranger to fuck me, and now I've got my lady parts in the air to keep his swimmers inside. "I mean, I don't know. I've never asked an alien to impregnate me before." More laughter bubbles up inside me. "This is definitely the weirdest night I've had in a while."

Ainar chuckles. "I am glad it is not just me feeling this is an unusual sort of request." He pauses and then blurts, "Not that I am not happy to help, because I am, Colonist Naomi."

"Just Naomi," I tell him. "And thank you. I know this must be really bizarre for you, but I didn't want to lose my money."

"Not bizarre," he says, and his voice gets shivery soft. Is... that his hand stroking up my thigh? My belly flutters with anticipation. "May I confess something?"

"Of course."

"I could do that again," Ainar blurts. "If you wish to be certain. Fill you with seed, that is." He pauses, and I can practically hear him swallow. "Unless you found it unpleasant. Found *me* unpleasant."

My body clenches in response. "You...you want to go again? Already?" The man just barely took a few breaths and he's ready for round two?

"Is that a problem?" He sounds anxious. "I thought it would be a good thing."

"It is! No, it absolutely is. I would love to do that again." My body flushes with heat at the thought. "Can we put my legs down though?"

"Yes. Of course." Ainar hesitates, and then his hand skims down my leg slowly. It feels warm and hard and pleasant, and it's been so long since I've had gentle touches that I moan. "What can I do to make you come?" he asks. "Will that—will that help you make a baby?"

"Can't hurt," I breathe, reaching for him when he hitches

my legs around his waist. His cock presses up against the slick heat of my pussy, and I suck in a breath. "Not required, but absolutely can't hurt."

"Then tell me how I can do it," he murmurs. "Tell me how I can make you come."

His words ignite a fire inside me. I wriggle on the table, and when he strokes the head of his cock through my folds again, I whimper. He grunts—a surprisingly sexy sound—and then pushes into me. I'm so wet with our mingled fluids that he glides right in, and then he's filling me again, making every-thing tight and delicious and full of friction.

I shudder and cling to his forearms—god, they're fucking huge—and arch, trying to get the sensation of those piercings and ridges to work their magic. Instead, it pushes his spur against my clit in a perfect way and I cry out.

Ainar freezes over me. "Bad?"

"Good," I choke. "Really good. That angle—"

In the next moment, he's ripping his tunic off over his head. He wads it up and then shoves it under my hips, lifting them up. One big hand angles me, and then he presses in again and I practically *wheeze* because his spur is tapping against my clit when he rocks forward, and it might be the best thing I've ever felt. "Better?"

"So better," I tell him. "So...yeah...good dick. Very good. A-plus. No complaints." I'm babbling now as he glides in and out of me, stroking like he's petting my insides.

His hand goes under my skirt and plants over my mound, his thumb brushing against the spot where my clit gets rubbed with his spur. "Ah," he says, as if this is all a puzzle he's figuring out as he goes. "Feels good there?"

He presses lightly against my clit and my legs jump. I gasp and then I'm coming, clenching and squeezing around the universe's best dick. I'm probably still moaning about his dick perfection and how good it feels, but then he's coming inside me again and I ripple with another orgasm and I sort of lose track for a long moment after that.

Panting, I slowly come to my senses to find that he's still on top of me, mostly naked now, and his hand is gripping the front of my tunic in a knot with a death grip. His skin is sheened with sweat, but his eyes are watching me with utter fascination, and when I sigh, he rocks into me again. Our joined bodies make a wet sound, I make a gaspy one, and he groans.

"Again?"

Did I know what I was getting into when I asked him to help me out? No, no I did not.

Do I have regrets? Also no. If this doesn't make a baby tonight, no amount of alien semen will.

FOUR

AINAR

Hours and hours later, the door to the custodial office opens at the front of the building and makes me remember exactly where I am.

All night, I've been balls-deep into the sweetest, most beautiful, most *cock-hungry* human colonist I've ever met. Naomi is as perfect as she is relentless, and no matter how many times my cock rises and falls, her touch never fails to elicit another round from me. Even now, I'm still atop her, her skin sweaty and her clothing discarded somewhere on Sinath's nearby desk. Everything on mine has fallen to the floor due to our repeated matings, and the floor underneath my boots is a little sticky with our leavings.

We've made an absolute mess and I don't keffing care, because cleaning up would mean moving away from her, and I don't think I can do that.

But the moment the door at the front slides open with a

chime, it reminds me that we're not in private. I tense, and underneath me (and around my cock) I can feel Naomi tense.

Kef. Someone's here. Someone's here, and I've got a woman sprawled over my desk, covered in my seed.

This is absolutely not in the custodial regulations.

I slip out of the warmth of Naomi's body, and immediately there's a wet sound as my seed spills out of her. I wince, shoving my cock into my trou (luckily they were still around my ankles) and activating the auto-fastener. "Wait here."

"What time is it?" she asks, dazed. Naomi draws her legs together as I grab my tunic and pull it over her head, covering her naked limbs with it. It fits over her like a tent, and the auto-fastener at the collar flashes, notifying me it's undone.

I ignore it. "Just before dawn. Khex is coming in for his shift." And thank everything in the universe that it's Khex and not Sinath, because then I'd never hear the end of it. "Let me ask him to give us a moment for privacy."

Her eyes go wide and she clutches the collar of my tunic to her neck. "Oh my god, are we in trouble?"

"No, of course not," I reassure her. "I will let him know I was simply assisting you."

Naomi lets out a sigh of relief and nods at me. "I'll wait back here, then, until it's safe to sneak out."

Good. I will talk to Khex and explain the situation, and then I will guide Naomi's sled home for her, since she is likely too exhausted to be a safe driver. My shift is over anyhow, and I would like to spend more time with her. Get to know her better.

After all, I'm half in love with her already. She's perfect.

I gaze at her as she eases one leg slowly off my desk, wincing as her foot hits the floor. We've definitely made a mess of the office, but I can't help but be pleased as I regard her. Naomi's thick dark hair is a mess, cascading over her shoulders and snarled at the back of her head. A few locks are damp with sweat against her brow, and when she yawns, it is the cutest thing I have ever seen. I want to bury my face into her neck and breathe in our mingled scents. I want to haul her into my arms and carry her out to the sled.

I want to shove my fingers back between her thighs and plug up the seed that is already trickling down her skin.

Instead, I give her one last quick smile and then race toward the front of the office, down the narrow hall and ensuring the door shuts behind me as I move to the front of the building. I'm very aware of wearing nothing but my trou and my boots. My hair is probably a mess, my horns smudged with fingerprints, and all of my tattoos on my chest are on display, along with the piercings through my nipples. I've never worn anything but my complete uniform, collar fastened to my neck, and Khex is sure to give me grief about the ugly tattoos covering my skin of brand names I enjoyed as a youth and a few sayings that I thought were tough-sounding. Now they just embarrass me.

Khex stands by the front desk, a steaming mug of tea in his hand. He frowns in my direction as I arrive. "Ashley said to tell you hi and she made some night tea for you. But I'm guessing you don't need it since the entire office smells like a keffing brothel. You want to tell me why everything reeks of cunt or should I go in the back and say hello to whoever is back there?"

"No," I say quickly, moving to stand in front of the door controls. "She will be embarrassed." When Khex tilts his head, I continue. "I was helping a colonist. That's all."

"Helping her take her clothes off?"

I pause. "Yes?"

He inhales sharply, then shakes his head and takes a big swig of his night tea. "I'm going to need to be more awake before I hear this." He takes another swig and then gestures at me with his finger, indicating I should begin.

So I do. I tell him about Colonist Flannigan—Naomi—and how her predicament meant that she needed assistance getting pregnant. And how I, well, assisted her. Repeatedly. All night long. On my desk. I don't give him specifics about her. Not the sounds she made when I thrust into her, or the way it felt to have her gloved around my cock. I don't speak of the fact that she wouldn't kiss me, or the way she breathed my name when I rested over her. The squeal she made when I pushed my seed back into her body with my fingers.

Those things are *mine*.

But I do tell him that she wanted a baby and needed assistance. That her fertility treatment window ran out quickly and she had no choice but to ask for assistance.

"Keffing fertility treatments," he groans, scrubbing a hand down his face and then shaking his head. "Those things cause more trouble than they're worth."

"They're worth it to the colonists, sir," I say stiffly, not wanting to feel disloyal to the female over at my desk, currently full to the brim with my release. "I think it's understandable for them to want a family when theirs has been taken from them."

Khex grunts. "I've a mind to tell Lord va'Rin that these medics are causing problems peddling their solutions under the table. But then if he makes them all leave the planet, my mate will kill me."

"Because she wants a child?" I guess. I've met Ashley and while she didn't seem as if she was pining for children, you never know.

"Because she wants the choice, and I won't take that away from her." Khex scrubs his face again. "All right, well, you said the situation is handled, right? Are you going to mate her? Do I need to cover your shift for the next few days while you two get yourselves sorted?"

My ears burn and I rub my chest, feeling a little ashamed. "Actually, she just wanted a donor..."

I trail off as the sound of a sled taking off hums from just outside. The only sled that close would have to be parked right in front of the custodial office, which means that Naomi has ran off without saying goodbye. And kef me, that hurts. I try not to keep a neutral face and not show my disappointment. She did make it quite clear what she was looking for.

I guess she got it and now she's done with me.

Khex averts his gaze and slurps his tea really loud.

"I...suppose she got what she needed," I say, stiff. "I am glad I could be of assistance to a colonist. To answer your question, no...I will not be needing time off."

The room is silent.

Sluuuuurrrrrrrrp. Sluuuurrrrrp.

I'm tempted to knock the mug out of his hands.

"You want some advice from an old pro when it comes to females?"

"You?" I give him a skeptical look, crossing my arms over my bare chest. "Did you not just mate your female a few months ago? I am not sure that qualifies you as a 'pro.'"

He just gives me a lazy grin and slurrrrrrps his tea again.

I clench my teeth. "Fine. Speak."

"I just want to point out that human females are not great communicators." He shrugs, leaning against the desk near the front and raising his mug to his lips once more. "My mate in particular? Keffing terrible at it. They never tell you what they want. They expect you to read their minds."

Pausing, I consider this. "Is mind-reading common on their planet?"

"No. Which is why it's so incredibly frustrating." He rolls

his eyes. "They're lucky they're so appealing. But I'm telling you this because you should assume that she is bad at communicating what she wants, like the rest of her kind. If you wish to see her again, you'll need to tell her. Get some flowers, show up on her doorstep, and tell her you had a good time." His nose twitches. "I mean, it's clear to me that from the reek of this place that you two were having a keffing *great* time."

"It was rather nice…" Is he right? Is Naomi like Ashley in that she will not share her thoughts? She will expect me to read her mind in some fashion? To automatically know what she wants? This makes things tricky. "You truly think I should do so?"

"Would you rather her walk away and be done with her?"

"Well…no."

Khex chuckles. "You're like every other mesakkah. The moment you see your female, you just know she's yours. I get it."

I might think Naomi's mine, but Naomi clearly doesn't feel the same way. She did not even stop to tell me goodbye. I clench my jaw, because it does no good to feel wounded about the situation. She was quite specific. "What if she is not interested in more?"

"Then you know for sure and you can move past things." He shrugs. "What can it hurt to throw things out there? Like I said, go tell this female you had a good time, and tell her *exactly* what you want. Be specific."

Be specific. Tell Naomi what I want.

I…think I can do that. I nod.

"Great. But I'd recommend cleaning your desk up before Sinath and Paxon get in." Khex's nose twitches again. "And I'm going to open a few windows."

FIVE

NAOMI

I absently suck on my lower lip while I steer my sled into the dusty "parking space" in front of my house. Instead of feeling accomplished, I'm all over the place. My emotions are everywhere, and that's not something I expected. This sex was supposed to be transactional. Just to make a baby. Ainar could have jizzed in a cup and gotten the job done, so I should not be thinking twice about him.

And yet...here I am, full of a stranger's sperm, wearing a stranger's tunic, and trying not to think about how I just had my brains fucked out by the intergalactic equivalent of a grown up Boy Scout. Except instead of helping me cross the street, he held me down and hammered into me until I came. And came.

And came. And came some more. I lost track of how many times we had sex. Seven? Eight? Ten? I know I'm feeling a little chafed and definitely well-seeded, which is the point. I should be focusing on what comes next...and instead I keep thinking about Ainar. Ainar and those big hands that were surprisingly gentle. Ainar and his four-way piercing dick, which felt far too fucking good. Ainar and his oh-so-awkward kiss.

We never did kiss, come to think of it. Maybe that's a good thing. I fight back a wave of disappointment at the realization, though. I'm just lonely. Of course I want to kiss a guy with a great dick and a caring attitude. No one's taken care of me for years now. If anything, I should feel guilty when I think about Ainar instead of wistful. The guy was just trying to do his job and here I dive-bombed him, insisting he fuck me.

I cringe at the thought. I probably came on *really* strong. I make a mental note to not show my face around town for a while, so I don't run into him and make things awkward. It'll take at least a week for me to be certain if things have "taken" so I can just make myself busy around the farm. Paint the barn. Wash the stalls. Clip the nails of the meat-stock. Make them special meat-stock vegetarian meals. Do whatever it is that farmers do when they've got a lot of free time.

With a sigh, I get out of the air-sled and brace myself. Sure enough, there's a migration of fluids south the moment I stand, and I feel a hint of panic. What if it wasn't enough after all? What if I need a few more swimmers to do the deed? Racing inside, I fling myself down on my bed. Lying on my back, I put my legs in the air and rest my heels on the wall, tucking a pillow under my hips to elevate them. I have no idea if this does anything, but they always did it in the movies back home, so it must, right?

Propping up my hips makes me think of Ainar, though, and the way he'd shoved his tunic under me to try and give me what I needed. I grab the collar of it and raise it to my nose, sniffing it like a teenage girl with a crush. God, I'm such a dweeb. You'd have thought that after the last five years, the universe would have beat all the silliness out of me, but it seems like I've still got some lingering. It's just...I'm allowed to indulge in a bit of fantasy, aren't I? It doesn't hurt anything. As long as my farm is running smoothly and I'm not hurting anyone, what's the harm?

So I let myself daydream about a big, hunky blue alien with ridges going up and down his thick cock (good god, was it thick), piercings and a spur. I must still be a little horny because my insides clench just thinking about him. I was prepared for bad sex. I was prepared for the indignity of a modified turkey-baster situation. I was not prepared for amazing dick. Maybe that's why I let myself get distracted and stayed all night long.

Well, the deed is done. I'll know in a week.

I tell myself I'll sit with my legs up for an hour, no more, and then go shower and check on the farm utilities. The bots normally have everything handled, but I make sure nothing gets hung up or stranded. Even the smartest bot isn't a replacement for good old-fashioned human oversight.

I'll do that soon. For now, I'm going to keep my hips elevated and think about Ainar for a little longer—

There's a knock at the door.

With an alarmed squeak, I fling my legs down and sit upright, finger-combing my hair. "Computer, show the porch please?" With my first harvest, I took all of my extra funds and sank them into a decent security system so I wouldn't be worried about living out here alone, and I'm grateful for it every day. The porch vid shows a large mesakkah in a Port Custodian uniform—a fresh one—and wet hair that's been combed back between his horns...and a bite mark on his neck that I probably left at some point last night. Ainar clutches a handful of flowers, and as I watch, his tail wiggles back and forth behind him as if he's an excited puppy.

It's that happy tail that makes me blush and tells me this isn't a simple "you forgot something at the station" visit. Ainar came after me? I was pretty specific that last night didn't have to mean anything at all...but maybe he misunderstood?

Smoothing my hair, I get to my feet and wince, because I still haven't showered. I'm still...well, I'm still wet in all the inappropriate and very sore places. I'm also still wearing his shirt.

Oh. Oh, maybe he came for it. He wants his shirt back. But then why bring flowers?

I straighten my clothing and then move to the door and open it. "Hi again." It's hard not to smile when his eyes immediately light up at the sight of me. "Is everything okay?"

Ainar thrusts the flowers toward me. "I wish to taste your cunt."

Um...?

At my blank expression, his falls and his tail goes still. "Was that inappropriate? Khex said I should be straightforward."

"It's okay. I was just surprised, that's all. So...was that like a greeting, or...?"

Ainar gives me a sheepish little smile, lifting the flowers and holding them out to me again. "I am trying to tell you what I want. I wished to say something at the office but I was distracted. And then you left, and now these things are unsaid. So I am trying to say them now."

I tuck a strand of hair behind my ear, feeling sweaty and disheveled and weirdly happy. "Do you want to come inside? Have breakfast? I just got home not too long ago and haven't even showered yet." I gesture at what I'm wearing. "Obviously."

"Are you all right?" he asks, and his tail starts to swing in that hopeful manner again. "Did I wear you out? Do you need help?"

He looks excited at the thought of helping me, but I feel a

little silly. "Actually I was putting my legs up for a little longer, just in case it was needed." My face feels hot. "We can talk over breakfast and then I should shower and look in on the animals."

"I will make you breakfast, if you like?" Ainar says with a smile. "I have some small skill with cooking."

"Oh, um, sure?" I take the flowers and give him a quick peek through my lashes. "You did hear me when I said you didn't have to stick around, right? That if we do make a baby I'm not wanting a father for it? I don't want you to feel obligated about last night in the slightest. It was just sex."

"I understand," he says, stepping inside. "Would you like noodles? Or pancakes? Rektar's mate Lucy taught me how to make human foods, and while I do not like eggs, I enjoy the other cakes you have for your morning meal. And I can make a good cup of night tea."

Night tea is nasty, bitter in a way that coffee isn't, but it's what people use here to caffeinate. "I'm not a huge fan of night tea, but yes to the pancakes? I have some ground meal that's almost like flour if you want to give it a try?" I wander toward my kitchen, trying to figure out what I'm going to put my flowers in. They're noli flowers, I think, which I've been told to be cautious with around praxiians, but there aren't any here, so it's a moot point.

"I shall ready everything," Ainar tells me cheerfully, and takes the flowers from my hand. "You can shower and I will ready a meal for you."

"Actually I should see to my farm first," I admit, and then sniff the borrowed shirt delicately. "Unless you're telling me I stink...?"

His eyes widen and then his mouth curls in a reluctant, almost shy smile. His tail goes back and forth like mad, though, as if it's showing all the emotions he's trying to hide. "You smell like me and mating. I would like it if you wore that scent forever."

Oh. I blush.

"Do you need help with your farm?" he asks.

"No, I'm fine. I can handle it." I move to the door and put my shoes on. "If you don't mind waiting a few minutes, I'll get things checked out."

He dips his chin in an eager nod. "I will make you a fine morning meal."

I can feel myself blushing again—a man is going to cook for me after we had a ridiculous amount of sex? I don't know what to think...just that I like it. But I bite the inside of my cheek so I don't grin like an absolute lunatic. "Be back soon."

Going out to the barn allows me to clear my head for a bit. It's not that the farm itself isn't almost completely mechanized. Bots run everything, from taking stool samples of the cattle for vitamin readings to herding to feedings, there's very little a human has to do. But even the best, most well-programmed bot gets stuck from time to time or malfunctions. I always check over everything because it's what I was taught. You can't rely on machines to do everything. You still have to be the brain behind the works. Sure enough, one of the feeder bots is stuck in the deployment chute, and several others are stuck behind it. The space cattle (called "meat-stock" by the unimaginative mesakkah) are gathered around the chute, lowing and bleating their displeasure. I wade in, pushing the hungry cattle aside, and free the bot from the chute. The others pour out immediately, and the cattle immediately follow them out to the feeding spots. A quick check of the chute shows that there's a tiny metal edge that's come up on one smooth side of the chute. I hammer it back down and then check the readings on the rest of my farm equipment before heading back in.

I've been so focused on the problem at hand that it allowed

me to clear my head and not obsess over Ainar and his reap-pearance. It's a good thing. It means I can try to think logically about his being here and what I want from him. He's made it pretty clear that he's interested in more than just last night's hook-up.

I'm not sure how *much* more. He might just want to get laid again. He might want to be my friend. He might want to be in the baby's life...if we've even *made* a baby.

I'm still awkwardly wet between my thighs and sweaty from last night, but my head feels clearer. I'm pretty confident I won't make any impulsive decisions...and then I laugh, because what in the entire universe can be more impulsive than grabbing a stranger and demanding he make a baby with me?

When I open the door to my house, delicious scents fill my nose. It smells a bit like apple fritters, which I didn't know I wanted until just now. My mouth waters and I wander into the kitchen, where Ainar is happily flipping a pancake, his tail wagging. He turns at the sight of me, a smile creasing his broad face. "Oh good. You're back. Are you hungry? Do you like *klischaar* fruit? I noticed you had a jar of it untouched and it goes really well with these things you call pancakes."

I move to the sink and wash my hands up to the elbow. "I don't know what that fruit is. Is it the stuff that looks like snot? Mary that lives two farms over moved away and the women divided up her canned goods. I ended up with that but I've been too scared to try it." I scrub up, trying not to think about how the rest of me needs a good scrubbing. Am I a heathen if I eat breakfast while wearing cum-filled panties?

Fuck it. Those pancakes smell too good.

Sitting at the table, Ainar puts a mug in front of me full of night tea and then plates several of the pancakes. "The fruit turns colorless when you cook it, so don't be surprised to get a few chunks of it in your pancake."

I take a cautious bite, and it does taste just like apples from home—a little more tart and unripe, but I could get used to the taste very quickly. The rich taste of the pancake sets it off nicely and I don't even need honey to top it. The edges are crispy from the griddle and it's the best thing I've eaten in a long time. "This is amazing," I tell him, raising a hand to cover my mouth. "Holy crap, you're a genius."

His tail wags harder, and I swear, you'd think he'd won a prize. "The tea is a recipe of mine, too."

I don't have the heart to tell him that I hate night tea, so I take a small sip of it...and it's a pleasant surprise. It's not nearly as bitter as it normally is. I give him a look of astonishment, and Ainar's face breaks into a huge grin. "What did you do to it?" I ask. "It tastes good!"

"Lucy—that's Rektar's mate—mentioned that she thought night tea was too strong. Back home my mother would always make her night tea with an *atsach* leaf in it. She had a bad stomach and didn't like the bitterness of the tea, and she said the leaf soaked up the bad taste."

"She's right," I tell him, drinking it with wonder. It reminds me of a rooibos tea from home instead of the burned char at the bottom of a coffee pot that's been on the burner too long. Still strong, but with a smooth taste instead of a hard bitter edge. "I love this."

"I am glad." He beams at me and then sits down across from me at the table, with one pancake on his plate. "I am trying to learn the things that humans like. Working as a custodian reminds me that not all races think the same, and of course we do not taste things the same, either. Lucy has taught me that. One day she made a very sweet cookie for all of us at the custodial office—she is always baking for Rektar. And

Sinath was the only one that could eat them. They were so sweet they made Paxon vomit." He winces. "Humans like very sweet things."

"And mesakkah do not?"

"We like a lot of flavors, but mostly savory ones." He takes a small bite of pancake and then blurts out, "I still would like to lick your cunt. I meant that."

I flush, shoving another bite of pancake into my mouth. "We should probably talk about this whole you and me thing."

His tail makes a sad thump against his chair, and his smile remains, but I just *know* his tail isn't wagging anymore. "Of course. Am I making you uncomfortable—"

"No," I say, eating another huge bite of pancake. I've worked up quite an appetite, it seems. I'm weirdly not tired, either. You'd think I'd be sleepy after last night's marathon pound-session but I feel pretty wired. "I'm not telling you to fuck off, by the way. I'm just trying to set expectations."

The look on his face is cautious. He nods, taking a sip of tea. When I eat the last bite of pancake, he discreetly pushes his plate over to me. "I am listening."

I eat his pancake, too. Because you don't let something that delicious go to waste. "The guy I initially hired was supposed to be a one and done sort of thing. No attachments, no nothing."

"I remember. You hired him to service you."

That last bite of pancake sticks to the roof of my mouth and I grimace. Did he have to use the word "service"? I wash it down with tea, then clear my throat. "I wanted it that way because a baby is a *commitment.* I'm fully aware that a guy might be fine with sex but not necessarily a baby. And after a few years of being a slave, I didn't want to have strings attached to another person, if that makes sense."

"You do not wish strings attached to me, then," he says slowly. "Strings are...relationships?"

"Yes. No. Kinda?" I wince, because I'm flailing at explaining this. "What I'm trying to say is that I didn't come to you last night because I wanted you here this morning. If you would have patted me on the back and said 'Thanks for the fun' and I never saw you again, I'd be okay with that. Does that make sense? But I do like you. And I had a good time last night. And I like that you're here this morning. I'm just not sure how to wrap my head around it all."

He relaxes, his smile returning. "So you are happy with a sex partner and a friend but I should not assume it to be more? And you do not wish for your child to have a father because he would put expectations upon you and you do not wish that?"

I blink, because he's summed it up rather nicely. "Actually, yes. That's it exactly."

"I understand. I did not come here to force my life upon you, Naomi." He gives me another one of those smiles that look like they'd be awkward and shy if he wasn't a seven-foot-tall horned alien with huge, veined biceps that could crush a skull. "I came here because I did not want last night to end. And I am here making a fool of myself because I like you and I wish to see more of you. If we take things beyond last night, I will let you decide how all things go."

"I...think I can do that." It feels strange to have him agree so easily. Shouldn't he be fighting to be the dad of my possible child? But maybe aliens do all things in a different way. It shouldn't be this easy, right? Relationships should be hard. Not that what we have is a relationship. I guess we're...fuck buddies? Breeding buddies?

Breeding buddies, I decide. That sounds about right. "So... what now?"

Ainar's tail starts to thump against the chair again and he

looks delighted. "I would like to know everything about you, Naomi Flannigan, including how you came to acquire your musical name. Were you born in the land of Flannigan?"

I bite back a laugh. "No, Flannigan is a family name."

"Ah, a house name." Ainar nods. "An important house?"

Important? "I honestly have no idea. Back on Earth, it's just a last name. Makes it easier to classify you and to separate you out from all the other Naomis that might be floating around."

"Then your people do not base your importance upon which house you come from?" He seems surprised by this.

"I mean, maybe some do? I think a few countries still have monarchies with old families. But where I come from, your importance is based on your wealth and education more than anything." I shrug. "Not that it matters now, because I'm here. Here, I'm just another colonist."

Ainar nods thoughtfully. He stares down at his mug. "My family name is vo'Lon. It is not a good one."

I can tell it bothers him. I'm a little concerned because he'd said his family name wasn't great, but I didn't think about what that actually entailed. What if it means he comes from a long line of serial killers and violent murderers? "Not good in what way?"

"We are refuse collectors. It is the only job allowed to my family line. That...or entering the military. Which is why I am here."

Oh. I relax at that. "That's a hard job and maybe not fun, but there's nothing wrong with it. Someone's got to do it. Job security, right?"

His smile returns reluctantly.

For some reason, it bothers me that he should feel bad about his family trade. "If you boil things down, every job can have an unglamorous side. Look at me. I play in the dirt and analyze cow poop for profit. Nobody back home would find this particularly exciting because it's a job that fulfills basic needs. But I'm good at it, and I made enough money for a baby. A *hopeful* baby, that is. And next time, maybe I'll add onto my house or get a new sled. Who knows."

He tilts his head, letting his horns indicate a direction. "I noticed that you have no crops in your fields this year. Was that deliberate or have you been having trouble?"

"It's deliberate, actually." I grin. "This year I'm letting the cattle graze in that particular field and letting them shit all over it to fertilize. Next year, I'll grow flowers. It's a good idea to rotate crops and let the fields go fallow, but when I was a slave for a cattle baron on another planet, he'd rotate his fields like so and always had good yields, so I'm following his lead." Fucker was good for something, at least.

"That is excellent to hear," Ainar replies with a nod. Then, he blanches as if he realizes what he just said. "It is not excellent that you were a slave. Just that your farming is successful."

"It's okay." I reach across the table, holding my hand out. "I know what you meant."

He takes my hand in his, his fingertips brushing over mine. He gazes at our linked fingers for a moment and then up at me. "So what happens now?"

"With the baby? I take a test in a week to see if it was successful. The doctor said he has a good success rate but it depends on a lot of factors." Just thinking about it gives me goosebumps. In a week, I could be pregnant. In a week, I could be a mom-to-be. In a week, I could have something to look forward to, something that would make each day a little brighter and less lonely.

Thump thump thump.

Ainar's tail. His smile is bright as he holds my hand. "I hope I was of help to you, Naomi."

I run my thumb over his big blue finger. His nails are

square but short and clean. He's callused and his palms are wide. They're not the elegant, long fingers of an artist, but the blunt tools of a working man. I decide I like them. I like them a lot. "Are you kidding? You absolutely saved my bacon. And before you ask, that means you saved the day. You rescued me and fixed the situation, and I'm so, so grateful to you."

His tail thumps harder against the chair, and the look he gives me is intense. "Grateful enough to let me lick your cunt?"

A tiny squeak of surprise escapes me. It's so blunt of him to state things like that, and yet...this might be the first time a man has ever begged to go down on me. "You...really want to do that?"

Ainar rises so quickly from the table that it almost flips over. He straightens it, his gaze locked on plates that have skidded to one side. "I would love nothing more, Naomi. I have been dying to touch you—pleasure you—since I met you. And I know last night was about making a baby, but now that we have time, I would like to kiss you." His gaze moves over me and his eyes are full of longing. "But only if that is what you want, too."

"I-I'm not opposed to it." What single woman being propositioned by a gorgeous, eager man would be? "But I still haven't showered."

His eyes light up. "I will wash you. I would *love* to wash you."

I thumb a gesture at the shower. "Um, okay. You...you wanna join me then? We can wash together and keep the conversation going." This is normal, right? Fuck a stranger, have him make you breakfast in the morning, then shower together? Then I tell myself that it really doesn't matter. Normal went out the window the day I was abducted by aliens. I've just been rolling with the punches ever since. "It's this way."

With a pair of fluffy towels from my linen closet, I lead the way to the small bathroom in my house. I shouldn't feel shy, I tell myself. He's seen me naked. He's practically rearranged my insides with that huge dick of his. He's come inside me more times than my last relationship. There's no reason to be nervous. It's just...bathing together is intimate and I just met him. It feels like something a tender lover would do, not a couple of strangers who fucked like madmen for an eight-hour period.

I glance over at Ainar. He follows behind me, his hand rising as if he wants to touch my back, and then he drops it just as quickly again. His tail is waving back and forth, though, wagging like he's happy. Excited. Fucking thrilled to shower with me.

It's that wagging tail that tells me that my nervousness is ridiculous. That even if he notices I have stretch marks on the insides of my thighs or one of my tits isn't quite as big as the other, it's not going to make that much of a difference. And if it does make a difference...well, it's not as if it's a long-term rela-tionship. I literally just met him.

My bathroom—what aliens tend to stuffily call a "lava-tory"— is small, but I never realized just how small until now, when Ainar crowds in next to me. He takes up all the space, our bodies bumping into one another next to the sink. He makes an awkward sound in his throat, and when I turn around to glance at him, clutching the towels, he looks shy again.

Our eyes meet and he speaks. "Should I—"

"No," I say, before he can try to talk himself out of this. "It's fine. Just a tight fit."

A smile creases his face and I wonder why anyone would pass him by. He's just so damn adorable. Like an oversized puppy with gargantuan hands and an enormous dick. Women on his planet are jerks, I decide. I set the towels down on the edge of the sink and put a hand on the fastener at the throat of his tunic. I'm still wearing his old one so this must be a fresh uniform. "Can I undress you? I didn't get to see a lot yesterday."

Yesterday? More like a few hours ago, I correct myself. And he did take off his tunic at one point, but it was because he was covering me up, and I wasn't paying attention to his bare skin.

He nods, his body stiffening as he holds still for me to explore. The only movement? That constantly swaying tail. I put a hand to his collar, high above my head, and activate it. The auto-fastener hisses and slithers down his front, opening up to reveal bits of tattooed blue skin. I peel his tunic back, revealing his chest...and the twin nipple piercings. Well now, that's interesting. I reach out and touch one, a little surprised to feel that his nipple is almost as hard as the piercing itself. They're not soft but firm like mine. "Did these hurt? When you got them pierced?"

"No. The tattoos on my hands hurt more."

"Do they have a lot of sensation?" I brush a finger over the ball studding one of them. They look similar to his dick piercings—the twin balls laced through the skin instead of a ring.

"Only when they are tugged on. I just liked the look of them. I...saw it in a vid once and was curious." His tail sways harder as I touch the other. "I admit they have been disappointing."

"Because they don't feel like much?" When he nods, I tug on one. "Are you not sensitive here?"

He shakes his head.

"Maybe you need a lot of sensation." I pull harder, then give the piercing a vicious twist.

Ainar gasps, his eyes going wide. That's what I thought. Any normal human would be screaming with pain right about now, but if his skin is thicker, his responses aren't going to be as sensitive. He's going to need to be rough. Or rather, I am.

The look he gives me is full of heat. Something prods against my belly and I realize his cock is growing, pushing out and crowding the small sliver of space between us. I reach down and caress him, then glance back up at Ainar. "I'm not going to pull on these, don't worry."

"Unless I ask?"

"Unless you ask," I agree, biting back a giggle. I think I've created a monster. "Can I finish undressing you?"

His gaze is hot on me and he nods.

I feel strangely sexy right now. Sure, I need a shower badly and my hair looks like a disheveled rat's nest. I probably have huge rings under my eyes. But Ainar stares at me as if he's watching a goddess at work and it's hard not to appreciate that. It makes me feel powerful. In charge.

I want more of that feeling. After a few years of being tossed around the universe like a leaf on the wind, I'm grabbing at any power I can. I like being in charge of my farm...just like I like the fact that Ainar lets me take control. Even though he's huge and strong, I've never felt threatened. I'm in charge and he's made that abundantly clear.

Stroking the hard bulge between his thighs, I smile up at him. "I might not want to have sex again, just so you know."

He gives me a very serious look. "I understand."

"I might not want to do anything except let you lick my pussy. I'm just letting you know in advance."

Instead of being offended, his tail starts to move faster. "But you'd let me lick your cunt?" When I nod, he grins with relief. "This is wonderful news. I accept."

I bite back another giggle. I accept. Like I'm giving him an award. *Congratulations, sir. You're this year's recipient of the Rights*

To Lick Naomi's Pussy Award. Please have your speech prepared. I like this guy. I like him a lot. I gaze down at the beast under his trou, fully outlined as I press my hand against the material of his pants. He's so hard and eager, I can practically make out the head of his cock—studs and all—against the fabric.

It reminds me that he's got piercings there, too. So many fascinating piercings, and tattoos, too. I activate the auto-fastener on his trou and they slither down his thighs. His cock practically springs free, and I stroke my hand over him again, this time skin on skin. He's got more tattoos on his hips, I notice, and they look like writing. "Are those words?"

He doesn't answer, and when I look up, Ainar is rubbing his ear, a sheepish expression on his face. "You should know I got most of these tattoos when I was young."

His embarrassment is adorable. "You're still young, Ainar. You're what…twenty five?"

"I am thirty."

That surprises me. He looks younger, but at the same time, I'm glad we're closer in age. "I'm thirty-two." I slide my hand from his cock, the blue-flushed head deeply colored and beaded with pre-cum, and touch one of the words on his hip. "What do they say?"

"Foolish things."

"You can tell me. I won't laugh."

He groans as if pained and then takes my hand. Pressing my fingertips to one word, he explains. "This one says 'I like i'Kimra noodles.' It was a contest back on Homeworld. I did not win."

I press my lips together, trying not to laugh.

"This one," he says, guiding my hand just above his groin, "says 'More than Adequate Male,' though the translation sounds weak in the human tongue."

Shit. My shoulders shake. If I laugh, he's going to be offended. I fight to keep the giggles in.

He moves my hand to the opposite hip, where a bold swirl of words is placed. "This one encourages anyone that views it to feast upon the biggest noodle of all."

I burst into laughter, unable to hold it back.

"Again, it was for a contest," Ainar tells me. I look up at him, my hand going to my mouth as I try to stifle my snickers, but he's smiling. "They are foolishness. A young male's head full of dreams and not much thought."

"What did they offer you if you won?" I ask, giggling. "A year's supply of noodles?"

He shakes his head. "A job off world. The winner would be brand ambassador and very rich."

I stop laughing. Instead, an ache forms in my heart. The young son of a poor family, looked down upon by others in his world, with the only job available to him the military or a trash collector? No wonder he covered himself in silly tattoos to try and win. It's not funny, not anymore. "Oh, Ainar."

"I am glad I did not win. I would not have met you." His tail begins another slow wag, his smile gentle and sweet.

He's killing me with that tail. I reach up and tweak one pierced nipple, tugging. "Play your cards right and you might get that big noodle feasted upon after all."

"I do not play cards, but I should be happy to learn if you would teach me."

Oh jeez. I chuckle again.

CHAPTER

SIX

AINAR

I rub my stomach and the foolish tattoos there as Naomi strips her clothing—*my* clothing—off and steps into the shower. She laughed at them, but who would not? Even I find them ridiculous. I could get them removed, but I have left them as a reminder of my idiot days as a youth, when I dreamed to escape Homeworld and the future that awaited me. They remind me that even when I get frustrated with my low rank in the military, or if I have a bad day, that things are always better now. I have a good job that allows me to help people. I am serving on a planet full of sunlight and greenery. I have met the most wonderful female who knows what she wants and has a plan to get it.

Reminders are good things, no matter how silly they look, because they let me appreciate where I am today.

I try not to ogle Naomi's body as she climbs into the shower and begins to wash off. Flashes of last night tumble through my mind, of the tuft of dark hair over her cunt, of the way her body stretched around my cock, of her smooth flanks and the way they gripped me tight when I was deep inside her. Her breasts seem full and bouncy to me, the tips a warm brown that contrasts with her lighter skin. Her hips are broader, her backside full and pleasantly curved. She steps under the water to wash her dark mane, slicking it back under her hands, and then looks at me, our eyes meeting.

"Are you just going to stand out there or are you coming in?"

I had been waiting, actually. Rektar's advice floats through my head, reminding me not to crowd a human, to give them room. Reminding me that they have been through terrible things and might not want to be touched, or pursued.

Kef, and here I am, shoving myself into her lavatory and staring at her naked body. "Should I go?" I blurt out. "I can? If you like? I showered after I left the office, so it is not necessary."

Naomi wipes water from her face. She looks me up and down, staring at my naked body with a frown. "You want to go?"

"No. Not at all. I would like to join you," I say quickly. "I would like to wash you, and then I would like to lick your cunt." I pause, and then add, "Repeatedly."

She squints at me. "O-kaaaay."

"But I do not wish to push you into something you're not comfortable with—"

Naomi makes a gesture with her hand, indicating I should approach. I take a step forward and she grabs me by the arm, tugging me into the shower with her. "If I wanted you to leave, Ainar, I'd say 'Please fuck off and go.' And if you didn't leave, I'd call your boss."

"That is an excellent plan," I praise her as I try to squeeze into the shower next to her. Truly, this small box must be human sized, because it cannot fit a mesakkah well. I have to hold my head a certain way so my horns do not hit the sides, and my tail is smacking against the wall repeatedly. One wrong step and I will slip and fall and crush her underneath me.

"I'm not going to break, Ainar." She looks over her shoulder at me, stepping under the spray again. "And you promised to wash my back." She hands me a cake of soap that smells strongly of flowers, perhaps too strongly. "I'll wash you and then you can wash me, deal?"

As if any sane male would turn down such an offer. "It is a deal."

"Turn around," Naomi tells me with a twirl of her finger.

I obey, presenting her my back. She sputters, giggling. "Your tail is getting water all over the place! Stop wagging it!"

And because my life cannot possibly get any better, she grabs my tail and gives it a squeeze. She touches it in the middle, away from the less-sensitive tip and not nearly as close to the nerve-ending-laden base. Even so, I groan and clutch at the wall even as my cock jumps, reacting to her touch.

It is silent for a long moment, and then Naomi's hand lifts from my tail. She puts one on the center of my back. "Did...did I touch you inappropriately, Ainar?"

"Tails are very sensitive," I manage, staring at the tile. Perhaps if I stare long enough, my cock will cease throbbing and I will regain control of myself. As it is, if she touches my tail again, I imagine myself spraying wildly like a fertilizer bot.

"Bad sensitive?"

I shake my head.

"Cock sensitive?" Her wet fingers skim down my spine, moving teasingly toward the base of my tail, and my cock reacts once more.

"Very similar."

"So…I guess I shouldn't offer to wash your tail? Would that make you uncomfortable?"

My lungs feel tight. All of me feels tight, as if my entire existence is waiting for her to touch me again. "It would feel…good."

A slick hand grips the base of my tail. I choke on my breath as my cock surges to life again. With a groan, I grip my shaft and stroke it, even as her hand pumps the base of my tail. She leans forward, pressing her wet, dripping body against my back as she works my tail, and I can feel the tips of her breasts skim the plating on my back. She murmurs hot, seductive words, but I cannot hear them over the roaring of blood in my ears. I work my hand up and down my length in frantic, jerky motions, desperate to come. Behind me, the female makes a sound, and then a soft set of fingers are brushing against my sac—

I explode with release, gasping for air as the orgasm rocks through me so hard that I see stars. All of my form seizes up tight, my sac feeling as if it is drawing up into my body itself. My seed splatters on the tile directly in front of me, making an absolute mess of her shower. After coming so many times last night, I thought I would have less, but it feels as if my sac is a never-ending well of release, and I just keep spurting as she rubs her wet form against my back and works me in lascivious, decadent ways.

Universe have mercy, this female has unmade me. Naomi is a goddess. A goddess with wet fingers and a giggle against my back as she gives my tail one final squeeze and then shifts in the shower, the water spraying over my buttocks. "I dropped the soap."

I look down and sure enough, between my large, splayed feet, her pink cake of soap rests next to one of my toes. "Allow me to retrieve it," I say, my tongue feeling thick and silly in my mouth. I feel good, though. Like I could float away in this shower on the trickles of water. Naomi can play with my tail as much as she likes, I decide. It is hers to toy with, just like my cock. Just like the rest of me.

I do not know how I manage to remain upright, yet somehow I do. I manage to somehow remain in control as I retrieve the soap and hand it back to her. She washes me with gentle, quick touches, exploring my body and commenting on our differences. The fact that humans do not have tails, but she likes mine. She has no plating, and no piercings except in a few spots in her ears, which have filled in. She once had a tattoo of a flower on her hip but it was removed when she was stolen by aliens. She talks a little bit about how I am her first mesakkah. Her last owner was not, and so she is unfamiliar with our piercings and the spur just above my cock, but she likes them.

"My apologies," I manage as I step into the spray of the shower, washing off the soap that will probably leave me reeking of flowers for the next several days.

"For what? How I got here? It's in the past." She shrugs, handing me the soap and then presenting me with her back. "I've had a good cry over it. I've had several years of crying, actually, but when I came here, I told myself I wasn't going to be a victim any longer. I'm not going to dwell on that part of my life. I want to think about the future."

She is brave. I want to tell her that, too, but I worry it will come out wrong. If she does not wish to talk about the past, I will not make her. I know what it is to want to make a fresh start. To leave everything behind and start over as a new person. I know that very well.

So I wash Naomi's lovely body, making note of every tiny mole on her skin, every scar, no matter how small, every dimple on her backside. I want to memorize all of it. I soap her up, and I make careful, silent note of what touches elicit excitement from her. She likes it when I wash her hair for her, my fingers rubbing against her scalp. She likes soft touches on her neck and down her spine. She likes her breasts touched, but only the tips seem to be sensitive, and the backs of her knees are ticklish. I let her wash herself between her thighs since I don't want to be demanding of her body, and when we're both clean, I hop out of the shower first and wrap a towel around her.

Her expression is a little shy when I towel-dry her hair. "I can get that, Ainar. You don't have to baby me."

"Is it unpleasant?"

"What? No, of course not." She chuckles, blowing a lock of hair out of her face with her breath.

"Good. Then I will continue." I gently towel her hair until the excess moisture is gone and then move down her body. Her scent is now that of flowers, but I must be getting used to the smell of them because I can scent her, too. There's a hint of arousal in the air and her nipples are tight. I rub the towel against her hips, my cock stirring, and when she presents one delicate-looking shoulder, I lick the droplet of water off her skin instead of toweling it. "May I lick your cunt now, Naomi?"

"I mean...sure? If you want to." Naomi sounds breathless, and the scent of her arousal overpowers the flower-soap. "I don't want you to feel obligated—"

I groan at the thought, even as I towel her legs down. I want to press my face against her dimpled backside. I want to bury my lips in the small of her back and just breathe in her scent. I want to lick her everywhere. I want to feel her hold onto my horns and use them to rub herself against my face. I want so, so many things. "Not obligated. *Delighted.* I have been dreaming of this moment all day, Naomi."

I wonder if she'd let me tongue her right here. I could sit

her upon the edge of the sink and tilt her hips toward me and just…feast. I'd have to stay on my knees in this cramped lavatory, but I would not mind as long as my face is buried between her thighs.

"Wanna go to bed, then?" Naomi turns, holding her hand out. "Come with me."

Biting back another groan, I follow after her, letting her lead me through her small house. I should pay attention to our surroundings, note the things I can do to help her out with her farm as her mate (if she wants me, that is) but all I can do is stare at her enticing backside and how it sways when she walks. Then we are in her private quarters, and she gestures at the small single bed that is not nearly big enough for a full-grown mesakkah, much less one with a mate sleeping at his side.

I will have to bring her a bed for both of us, I decide. For now, though, this will do. "You wish to do this here?"

"I mean, we don't have to—" she begins.

Before she can make excuses or hesitate, I sweep her up in my arms. Naomi weighs nothing, but she makes a startled sound just the same. I set her down gently on the bed and then fall to my knees in front of it, ready to worship. "I have dreamed of this," I confess, parting her knees with gentle, reverent fingers and spreading her open. "Ever since you left, I have thought of nothing but tasting you, Naomi. This is a dream of mine."

"It's been less than a day, Ainar."

"And?"

She lets out a shuddery sound and I can feel her legs tremble. "Who am I to mess with dreams?"

I run my hand down one calf, starting with easy touches, since she seems to be nervous all of a sudden. To think that we showered together and I tried to impregnate her last night. She fondled my tail and sac in the shower, and I kneel before her, naked. Yet now she is nervous? I wish she could realize just how momentous this is for me.

I am about to pleasure my *mate*. Because Naomi is mine. I know that more with every second I spend in her presence. "If you tell me to stop, I will stop," I promise her. "I will never joke about such things or try to coax you into saying 'yes.' Your 'no' is very important to me. Understand?"

She nods, her eyes wide as she watches me.

"May I breathe in your scent first?"

"Sure?" Naomi sounds a little confused, but my request makes her relax. She eases a bit, and I take her foot in my hand and lift it to my nose.

I breathe in her scent, sniffing her ankle and the arch of her foot.

Wild giggles break from her, and she puts a hand to her mouth. "Sorry! Sorry!"

My lips twitch at her nervous laughter. "Did I do something funny?"

"I'm just wondering if you're secretly a foot guy. If you are, that's cool. It's just unexpected." Her cheeks are flushed with amusement, her eyes sparkling.

A foot guy? Does she mean a cobbler? I shake my head. "I have no secret jobs, Naomi. I am merely a custodian for the settlement, sent here by the military. I do not have time to make shoes."

Her brows furrow, and then she snicker-snorts with more laughter. "No, silly. I meant you're a *foot* guy. That you get off on sniffing my feet or something."

"I probably could," I confess. "But I think I would rather lick your cunt more than sniff your foot. I think I am a cunt guy." Yes. This seems right.

"Oh," she breathes, and her laughter dies away, replaced by a soft look in her eyes. "Yeah, that's fine, too."

"I am just breathing in your scent because I want to memorize it," I tell her, and run the tip of my nose up her calf. I do not tell her that I have noticed her nervousness, and that is why I am taking my time and breathing in her scent. I want her arousal scent to return, not her nervous laughter. If it takes toying with her feet for a bit longer, I shall happily do so. "Tell me if it troubles you."

"No trouble."

I lift her leg a little higher, and she reclines back on her elbows, watching me as I sniff her leg. And because she smells so sweet and lovely, and her skin looks so soft, I cannot help but press my lips to the inside of her thigh.

Naomi makes a low noise in her throat.

"Still good?" I ask, making certain.

"Still good."

"Excellent, because you smell much better up here." I continue to rub my nose along the inside of her thigh, heading toward the apex of her, where her scent is strongest and that tuft of dark hair calls my name. Her thighs quiver when I press my lips to them again, and when I glance up at her, Naomi's nipples are tight, her lips parted as she watches me. "You can touch me," I offer. "My horns will make excellent hand-holds."

I have heard Lucy joke about that with Rektar in the past, and now I cannot get the thought out of my head. I want Naomi to do that with me. I want her to steer me toward her pleasure.

Naomi makes another wordless sound but doesn't reach for my horns. Not yet, then. Strange how she can be so bold when it comes to demanding that I impregnate her yet the moment this becomes about her pleasure she grows shy. Her pleasure is just as important as mine, if not more so, because if she is not aroused, my desire will wither quickly.

So I take her hand in mine and plop it onto my horn. "Show me what you like. Steer me if you must. I cannot read your mind though I would dearly love to."

She makes another one of those shy sounds. The hand stays on my horns, but the other flutters toward her belly, and then lower. One finger slips between her folds, revealing a button of flesh. "This…is sensitive."

Ah, it makes sense now. How she'd whimpered when my spur pushed against that particular spot. I had not realized until just now how perfectly our bodies work together. I lean in and lick the small bit of flesh, and she whimpers like she did last night. "What is it called? A female spur?"

"No, a clit. Clitoris."

"And it is the most sensitive spot in your body?" I lick it again, eliciting another sound from her.

"N-not quite. Easiest…one to reach," she pants.

"May I see the others?" I lift a finger, slicking it through her folds. She's wet—so wet—that it makes me ache. I drag my finger up and down, teasing her cunt, and when I reach her clit, I rub it. She shifts her weight so I touch the side and not the bit of flesh directly, which I make note of.

"Other is inside me," Naomi manages. "Below…clit. Inside."

I study her body and then send an exploring finger deep inside her. Concentrating, I study her clit and its placement on her body, and try to find a similar spot inside her. Sure enough, the moment my fingertip brushes against a rough patch on her inside wall, her legs twitch and she whimpers again. "Found it."

Perhaps I should not be so smug with pride, but I like the thought that I am uncovering all of her spots, all of her secrets. I want to know just how to make Naomi feel good. I lick her clit again, teasing it with the tip of my tongue, and she arches against my hand, panting. "Oh god, *Ainar*."

I like the way she says my name. I lick again, tickling my finger against the inside of her body. I am tempted to push my tongue inside her, to see if I can lick deep enough to touch her inside-clit, but I do not think I can. So I concentrate on the outside one instead, lapping and teasing with my tongue while rubbing that spot inside her. Naomi makes small whining sounds in her throat, and her other hand goes to my horns. She pushes her hips up against my face as I work her, and I love that she is *using* me. My mouth is wet with her delicious taste, my face in her cunt, and I do not think I have ever been so keffing happy.

"Suck," she pants. "Suck on my clit. Need to *come*."

Oh, I can suck on it? I love her instructions, because I want nothing more than to please her. I close my mouth around the small bead at the apex of her cunt and suck, teasing the underside with my tongue. Naomi squeals, her hands tight on my horns, and she nearly bends in half, overcome with sensation. I love this. Biting back a groan of my own, I suck harder, working my finger inside her as I do.

A moment later she shudders, and Naomi rewards my efforts with a burst of fresh wetness as she comes. Delighted, I lap at her cunt in deep, delving strokes, wanting to steal every taste of her for myself. Pleasing her is amazing. Incredible. I want to do this over and over again.

I wonder if I can continue even now. I press her leg forward, pushing it toward her chest, and spread her cunt wider as I do, licking her with the flat of my tongue. She quivers with each stroke, moaning and bucking against me. A moment later, she comes again, her cunt clenching tight around my finger even as she chokes out my name. Excited, I suck on her clit again, wondering how many times I can repeat this.

"No," she moans, trying to clamp her thighs shut. "No no no, too much—"

Oh. This, I understand. Sometimes after I came inside her, my shaft felt too sensitive to touch. It quickly faded, of course, but if she needs me to abandon my efforts for a time, I shall. I pull away, pressing a kiss to her thigh before licking my fingers clean of her taste. Kef, I love all of it. "May I hold you at least?"

Naomi holds her arms out and I slide onto the tiny bed with her, adjusting our bodies so that her legs are on the mattress. Mine have to bend in half so I can fit, and my backside hangs off the edge of the bed, but she is curled against my front, her damp hair pressed under my chin and her slight body tucked against mine. I hold her close, wanting to shower her with affection, to nuzzle her and wrap her in blankets and feed her and tend to her...I want to do everything.

Her small chuckle rouses me from my thoughts. "You have an enormous boner, sir."

I do my best to remain still as she shifts her weight, rubbing her backside against me. "Apologies."

She laughs again, adjusting one of my hands so I am clasping her full breast. "Don't apologize. I like that going down on me turns you on."

"Does...is it not supposed to?" I am skeptical how any male can bury his face in his female's cunt and feel her shuddering with release and not feel *anything.*

She gives a little shrug. "Some men don't like that sort of thing."

"Then it is clear I will have to do twice as much to make up for their lack of enthusiasm." The thought fills me with joy, and my tail flicks happily. "Tell me when you would like for me to pleasure you again."

Naomi gives a breathless laugh. "Let me catch my breath? We can just talk for a while."

"I like talking," I agree.

She folds her arm over mine, snuggling back against me. "I know it's early in the day but if you're not busy, wanna spend the night again?"

My heart feels like pure sunshine. "I would love nothing more."

CHAPTER
SEVEN

AINAR

I have the pleasure of staying with Naomi that night and making breakfast for her again the next day. She eats the pancakes I cook for her with enthusiasm, and then we kiss before I head off to work. I have never kissed before, and the tangling of tongues and tasting of each other is so exciting, I arrive at work late, because I cannot stop kissing Naomi. I want to return to her bed and tongue her mouth, her breasts, her cunt, her everything…but I know Khex will be waiting for me at the custodial office.

To my chagrin, it is not Khex waiting, but Rektar instead.

His nostrils flare at the sight of me as I stumble into the office, and I worry that I smell of matings. Repeated matings. I showered this morning and Naomi worked my cock with her hand until I came. Is that what he smells? Chagrined, I nod at my boss. "Apologies for my lateness. I was…occupied. It will not happen again."

"It's not your lateness that concerns me," Rektar says. He

doesn't get up from his desk but folds his hands in front of him, and I feel like a young stripling back at school, waiting to be scolded by my teacher. "It's the fact that you come in wearing a wrinkled tunic and smelling like roses."

My eyes widen. Naomi's soap. Kef. I'd gotten so used to the stink of it that I didn't realize that it was clinging to me. Mesakkah have sensitive noses, and of course my boss would notice a floral scent. His mate is human and probably uses the smelly human soaps as well. I smooth my hand over the collar of my tunic, trying to straighten it. "Apologies—"

Rektar raises a hand in the air, shaking his head. "Khex tells me you had an encounter with a colonist who wished assistance in getting pregnant."

Heat suffuses my face. "Does everyone know, sir?"

"Everyone does," Rektar says flatly. "Sinath won't keffing shut up about it. Please tell me your version of events."

I do. Rektar's expression is disapproving right now, but I've worked for him for well over a year now and I know him to be fair. He will not judge me harshly. After all, he has a human mate as well. So I tell him about Naomi and her predicament, and how we mated, and how I wanted to see her again so I went over to her farm and we ended up in bed together again.

By the time I'm done, Rektar has his hand on his face, and the tip of his tail is slapping against the floor with irritation. "Khex advised you? I should have known." He straightens, rubbing his hand down his entire face and giving me a belea-guered look. "I know you mean well, Ainar, but I have to ask you. Is it possible that you're misinterpreting the female's interest?"

I swallow hard. "In what way?"

"Just that you pursued her after she got what she wanted. She told you quite clearly that she was not interested in a relationship or a father for her child, but you went over to her farm anyhow, correct? And showed up determined to woo her?"

My lungs feel as if they're being crushed in my chest. He's right. Naomi tried to leave—she slipped away and I followed her. She wasn't the one that contacted me. I went to her. "I think I see what you are saying, sir."

"I'm not saying that you're in trouble," Rektar says, his voice kind. "I'm just saying that humans are sometimes afraid to tell us what they want. They might say 'yes' when they truly mean no. Look at what they have come from. As those with a position of power in this settlement, we must be extremely certain that we're not abusing that power. Do you understand?"

I'm devastated.

He's right. Of course he's right. How many humans have I seen that skitter away from the sight of an alien male? That tell us that everything is fine when it is clearly not? So many of them are still in survival mode, saying whatever is necessary to get out of an uncomfortable situation. I felt like Naomi was stronger than that, that she knew her own mind better than that, but what if I'm wrong? What if all she truly did want was my seed? What if she was just humoring me when I showed up because she didn't know what else to do? She couldn't call the authorities, after all.

I am one of the authorities. She wouldn't expect them to protect her from me.

I'm silent, my tail limp. I don't know what to say. Shame infuses me. Shame and self-loathing.

"I could be wrong," Rektar says in a careful voice. "And if I am, I apologize. But for now, I think it's best that you let her initiate the next contact, Ainar. If she wishes to truly be with you, she will pursue you, not the other way around. Understand?"

I nod. He's right. If Naomi wants to see me, she'll contact me.

Until then, all I can do is wait and hope that she felt what I did. That I didn't just make the biggest mistake of my life. That I didn't hurt her when all I wanted to do was love her.

I want her for my mate, but if she doesn't feel the same...

If she doesn't feel the same, then nothing else matters. I'll leave the planet. Ask for another outpost. Get as far away from her as I can so she doesn't feel pressured when I'm around.

It's the least I can do.

EIGHT

NAOMI

One Week Later

Men suck.

"You ready?" my friend Martina asks as I hop up on the table at the clinic. She assists the local doctor after hours, handling a lot of the "human emergencies" since the doctor himself doesn't want to be troubled with them. He's kind of a dick, but I don't care. Martina will help me out.

"Hit me with it," I say, waving her on with a hand. "I can handle whatever the results are."

She gives me a wry grimace. "Fingers crossed that you'll have an easier time than I am."

I don't say anything to that. Martina has paid for four shots now and all four failed. Recently, her praxiian boyfriend left the planet and hasn't been seen in months. Something tells me he's given up on Martina, but she won't say anything about it. I haven't pried, either. Some things you just don't want to talk about with anyone.

Like the fact that my mesakkah boyfriend abandoned me after declaring himself. What the fuck is wrong with men? You don't show up with flowers, raving about how you want nothing more than to eat a girl's pussy and then ghost her. Here I'd thought Ainar wanted to get to know me. That after a couple rounds of earth-shaking sex and some awesome cuddling that we could see if there was anything between us. That maybe him and I had potential.

Nope. He's just like every other shitty man on this end of the universe. He hit it and quit it.

Martina holds the wand against my arm and a needle flicks out, jabbing me just enough to draw blood. "Ow!"

"Don't be a baby," she tells me as the needle disappears, replaced by a small suction pipe that pulls away the droplets of blood and leaves a tiny hickey behind on my skin. "Blood's the easiest reading here. I told my boss that back home humans peed on a stick indicator and he looked at me like I was crazy. Said we were disgusting and unsanitary creatures." She makes a face. "So I licked the rim of his mug when he wasn't looking. I hope he likes human cooties, the bastard."

I chuckle, my hand going to my belly. "I haven't felt anything yet," I confess. "I don't even feel different."

"It's too early for you to feel anything," Martina replies, studying the readouts on the machine. She gives me a side-ways look. "Or so I'm told." She holds the indicator out to me. "See that goofy-looking little character on the screen? That's the base hormone stuff for human females. If you're pregnant it's going to double and show a second character."

We both stare at the screen, waiting for the results.

"I take it you found someone to help you out?" she asks politely, watching the screen. "Was he nice? Single?"

"He was nice." My voice is soft, and even though it hurts to think about Ainar, I did tell him I wasn't interested in a relationship. He's just giving me what I wanted. I can't blame him. No guy wants to be made a dad unless it's his idea.

"Decent in the sack? Didn't give you trouble?" Martina sighs, leaning against the table. "Maybe you can give me his contact information if this works. God knows I could use a winner."

I eye her, hating that I'm jealous. I shouldn't be. Ainar abandoned me and never called me back, never said thank you for the sex, no nothing. And isn't that what I wanted? No strings attached? It's just...when he showed up the next day with eager eyes and flowers...I allowed myself to hope. That maybe this could be something between us. That maybe he was as good a guy as he seemed. That maybe I wouldn't be so lonely on this end of the universe. I could have a friend. A life partner. A lover.

"Oh, there's your answer," Martina says, showing me the screen.

I stare. And stare. And stare, trying to process it.

Then I glare at the readouts, suddenly angry. Fuck. I hop off the table and glance out the window at the innocuous gray building across the street, the Port Custodial Office. I bet Ainar's there.

And I've a sudden mind to tell him what I think of his disappearing act, the fucker.

If nothing else, he deserves to know the results of the test. Tears flood my eyes. Stupid, stupid tears. And even though I told myself I was going to be okay with the results no matter what, I can't stop crying.

CHAPTER
NINE

AINAR

I am miserable.

I've always considered myself a cheerful person with a desire to help others, but after a full week without Naomi in my life, I've never felt lower.

Rektar was right. If she'd wanted me in her life, she would have contacted me. The fact that she did not tells me that she is glad to be done with me. That she has never wished for my presence and that I foisted it upon her. It makes my heart hurt painfully. Even if she does not want me, my heart considers her my mate. It takes everything I have not to drive past her farm when I am done with my shift just so I can check in on her. I want to ask every human that comes to the custodial office if they have seen her and if she is doing well. I want to buy gifts and just have them sent to her farm to help her out. She does not even have to know it is from me.

I do not do these things, though, because if all she wants is to be left alone, then I must honor it.

71

But I truly am miserable. I have not washed the tunic I wore from her house. Sometimes I bring it out and breathe in its scent, hoping to catch a whiff of her instead of just flowers. I wonder if she has found out if she will be having a baby or not, or if it's too early to tell.

I wonder if she thinks of me.

All my joy has disappeared. Rektar gives me a kind pat on the back when he sees me, and Lucy has been bringing extra baked treats for me to try and cheer me up. I know that this will not be forever. That eventually this pain will fade and I will go on.

But I wonder if I should leave Risda entirely. Find another outpost so I do not chance running into Naomi and stirring up old hurts. More than anything, I want her to feel safe here, and perhaps she will not until I am gone.

I stare at job postings on my data pad. Most of the things I qualify for involve remote outposts in space, very few of them planet-side. One is for custodial work on Tarka V, a well-known refuse and recycling planet. A garbage posting. Even when away from Homeworld, I can't escape my heritage. With a sigh, I type in my identification to apply for the job.

The door opens to the front, the computer chiming to alert us that someone has arrived. "Your turn," Sinath says without looking up from the game he plays on his data pad.

"Welcome to the Port Custodial Office, Colonist Flannigan," the computer intones. "Someone will be by to assist you shortly."

Alarmed, I jump to my feet. Naomi? She's here? I shove my data pad behind my back and give Sinath a frantic look. "You must take this one. She will not want to see me."

"Me?" He glances at the direction of the front office, hidden from our desks by a long hall.

"Please," I say, my stomach tight. "She will not want to see me—"

Before I can finish my statement, a head pops around the corner and I see Naomi's dark hair and her expressive eyes. She searches the room and then her gaze lands on me. To my horror and yearning, she gets a determined look upon her face and strides toward me.

I can do this, I tell myself. I can be professional. She needs assistance, nothing more. She is seeking me out as a friend, someone that might be able to help her out with whatever she needs. Perhaps it's farm issues...

But as she approaches, I can see her eyes are red, her lashes spiky. Naomi has been crying.

Oh no. Oh no. I wasn't enough for her. I realize why she's here now. She is here to berate me and point out that my seed was not enough to make her pregnant. That she has wasted her credits. "Naomi," I breathe as she marches toward me. "I'm so sorry. I wish I had been enough for you."

She walks right up to me, defiance in her eyes. Her chin lifts and she looks me up and down. "I just want you to know that you walked out on a good thing."

I am...confused.

"I'm a good woman, and I'm not saying I'm the smartest or prettiest—"

"But you are," I blurt, unable to stay silent.

"—but I'm clever enough to make some credits and run my farm and make a profit." She crosses her arms over her chest, scowling up at me. "So you lost out. That's all I'm saying." She gives a hurt sniff. "So screw you."

"I am indeed screwed," I agree, though I don't know what it means entirely. Just that she is miserable and I understand. She blames me for the failure. "I will be leaving the planet so you no longer have to face me and my failure. I wish to make this as easy as possible for you, Naomi. You have my sincerest apologies, and please know that the nights we spent together were the happiest of my life." I want to reach for her hand, but I'm not certain that would be allowed, so I just bow slightly. "But I will accede to your wishes."

Naomi blinks up at me, her brows furrowed. "What the heck are you talking about?"

"I am sorry I was not able to make you pregnant," I say in a low voice, determined not to let the too-curious Sinath overhear. "I have failed you, but I wish for you to know that our time together was very enjoyable for me."

Her head tilts, and she gives me an odd look.

Perhaps enjoyable is not a strong enough word? "It was everything to me," I confess. "In my time with you, I have never been happier. I will cherish those memories forever."

Her lips purse, and I wonder for a moment if she is going to spit upon me. "You know what? I don't get you," she finally says. "I keep telling myself to give you understanding, that we're from alien cultures and that maybe there's some sort of custom I'm unaware of, but this is just taking the cake."

Taking the cake? Taking it where? I glance around, but I see no cakes, just the muffins that Lucy made earlier. Snatching one up, I offer it to Naomi.

"Can you please be serious? I didn't come here to be mocked."

I'm shocked she would think that. "I would never make fun of you. *Never.*"

She pauses, and there must be something in my voice that makes her believe me.

Sensing an opportunity, I continue. "I know I did not please you with my efforts, and I am sincerely sorry. I wish I could have done more for you, I truly do. You are..." I hesitate and then decide to blurt it out, because it doesn't matter. I am leaving, after all. "You are *perfect*, Naomi, and I am honored that you chose me."

Her mouth wobbles and her glare becomes fiercer. "You say that, but then you *ghosted* me." At my confused look, she pinches the bridge of her small (charming) nose. "Right. Let me try again. You left and never called me back. Never showed up again. You just vanished."

"I have been here the entire time," I tell her, confused. "I cannot abandon my post."

"Yes, but you left *me*," she emphasizes. "You brought me flowers and wooed me and then just—" She flicks a hand in the air. "Vanished. What am I supposed to think?"

With dawning understanding, I reply, "I thought if you wished to see me again, you would contact me. That perhaps I was forcing my attentions upon you and I should back off."

"You don't back off after flowers," she protests, giving me a strange look. "You don't back off after making me breakfast! You *call* me! You pick up your data pad and send me a note, or you comm me. You let me know what's going on in your head, Ainar, because what am I supposed to think?"

I pause, digesting this. Rektar told me to be careful with her, to let her re-approach, but I can also see how she was expecting me to approach her. Perhaps I should have pushed back against Rektar's suggestion. Naomi would not have invited me into the shower with her if she wanted me to leave, would she? She would not have been the one to reach for my cock and pleasure me if she wanted me to leave her alone. Rubbing my ear, I feel more than a little foolish. "I wonder that we should have perhaps had a conversation."

Naomi's laughter bubbles up. "You think?"

A hesitant smile curves my mouth, and my heart feels light. So light. "Then you do not feel I was being too pushy with my attentions?"

Her hands go to her hips and she gazes up at me. "Who was the one that walked in and demanded to be impregnated? If anyone's too pushy for attention, it's me. And you were a perfect gentleman. Any other guy would have tried to get his dick sucked, not showed up at my house to eat me out."

My mouth goes dry at her words. While I would never have presumed… "I am not opposed to getting my dick sucked—"

"Me too," chimes in Sinath, from behind me.

I bite back a growl. We'd forgotten that he's nearby, listening to everything. Turning, I glare at him over my shoulder even as I pull Naomi closer to me, hiding her from him with my bulk. "We are trying to have a *private* conversation."

"This office isn't private," Sinath points out. "I realize you're treating it as your own personal breeding station, but some of us have to work here, you know."

Keffing arse. I scowl, wanting to grab him and shove him out of the room. Naomi's lips twitch with amusement, though, and I decide I have a better idea. I take her hand, glare at Sinath as I lead her out of the back of the office and into the front, and then set her down at the table we first met at. Normally this is a place where we can consult with humans that require help, but I am using it for my own selfish needs today. I make sure Naomi is seated before I sit across from her and take her hand in mine. "Please ignore him," I tell her. "Sinath is highly, highly jealous that I was on call that night and he was not."

Naomi wrinkles her nose. "Is it rude if I say I'm glad you were on call, too? He's not my type."

My heart pounds. "What is your type, if I may ask?"

"Tall and blue, with a lively tail," she begins.

I immediately worry, because her description could be any mesakkah. I am not special to her.

But then she laces her fingers in mine and leans in.

"Someone kind. Someone that has to be persuaded to take advantage of a girl, even when she's begging him. Someone that isn't afraid to do hard work to get what he wants. Someone who keeps ridiculous noodle tattoos on his belly because they remind him of where he came from. Someone who makes a mean pancake—that's good, by the way—and lets me play with his tail as much as I want."

My chest feels warm with affection. "Naomi, I must confess something to you."

"Go on."

I move in close and whisper over our joined hands. "Most males would let you play with their tail."

She giggles, tapping my hand with her free one as if to tell me that she likes my joke.

I squeeze her fingers lightly in mine, wishing I could grab all of her and hold her against my chest. "Are you telling me that you like me? I want to be certain."

"I am."

My smile feels as if it is swallowing my entire face, it is so broad. My tail thumps against the stool I sit upon and this moment is almost perfect. Almost. My smile fades, and I remember the real reason she came here. "I am sorry I failed you, then. Please give me another chance."

Her expression changes to one of confusion. "Isn't...isn't that what this conversation is about? Me giving you another chance despite you ghosting me?"

"I meant the baby," I tell her. "I regret that I did not succeed for you. I know you wished for a baby more than anything."

"Oh. That." Naomi grins and pulls her hands from mine. "Actually I came over to tell you that I *am* pregnant. It did work."

"But...you were crying. I thought you wanted a child."

She laughs again, and her eyes are suspiciously damp. "I do. I was crying because part of me didn't expect it to happen, and then I was so mad at you for being a jerk."

"I am a jerk," I breathe, amazed, and try to remember all the things she has called me. "A ghost and a cake and I take the screw. I am all these things." When she starts to laugh, I know I have messed the words up, but I do not care. "Naomi, this is wondrous. You will have a child. I am so happy for you." I want to grab her and pull her into a hug, but then I get a better idea. "May I kiss you?"

"I'd be mad if you didn't," she tells me with a tearful giggle. Naomi gets to her feet before I can and flings herself into my arms. She presses her lips to my face, giving me short, delighted smacking kisses. "You big ridiculous man. Next time you have questions about anything between us, come to me first, all right?"

It sounds logical. But already I have a question. "You say 'us.' What are we?"

That makes her pause. She cups my face in her hands, standing between my thighs and gazing down at me. "That's an excellent question and one I'm not sure I have an answer for yet. Maybe we start with friends and see where that leads?"

This seems fair. But again, I have questions. "Do friends kiss?"

"These friends do," she says with a chuckle, and presses her lips to mine. "These friends can go to my house and have sex again, if you're so inclined."

I bite back a groan, because I love that idea. But... "I must finish my shift first."

She nips at my lower lip, using her teeth, and my body tightens with pleasure. "Then I'll come to your place after you get off work. Tell me the time and your address and I'll bring dinner. We'll celebrate the baby."

I like this idea. I like this idea a lot. "Done."

Naomi pokes a finger in my chest. "If you stand me up again, yes we are."

I do not care if corsairs invade the planet or a rogue asteroid hits—nothing is going to prevent me from meeting up with Naomi tonight.

TEN

NAOMI

Several hours later, I've showered, fixed my hair, put on my prettiest tunic, and picked up a casserole from the woman in town who likes to cook for others in exchange for credits. I park my air-sled in front of the building that Ainar programmed into my vehicle and step out. While I know there are a lot of people that work on the utilitarian side of Port—cargo shippers, dock workers, the military custodians —I never thought much about where they lived until now. There's a building close to the space port docks that looks more like a squat warehouse than an actual apartment building, but this is the place.

I let the door scan my palm and then step inside. To my surprise, there are stairs going down. Instead of a high-rise sort of building, this one goes into the ground. Huh. I lean over the railing, noticing doors lined up along the halls. Apartment doors. A szzt man in a dock worker uniform comes out of his apartment and I immediately tense, shivering, and press against the wall behind me. Szzt scare me with their casual cruelty. Their culture is a little sociopathic compared to humans, and a girl I was enslaved with used to joke that the only thing they taught szzt in school was how to pull the wings off flies.

My old master was szzt. I hope he's burning in hell somewhere.

"Naomi?"

I give a little scream of horror as a hand touches my arm. Turning, I see Ainar and breathe a sigh of relief. "Holy shit. I nearly flung noodles down the stairs," I tell him, holding up the disposable plas casserole dish. "Warn a girl, will you?"

The szzt male nods at Ainar as he passes us, heading out of the building, and Ainar stands close to me. Almost uncomfortably close, but I like it, because it makes me feel safe to have him pressed up against me. When the man is gone, Ainar turns back to me and gives me an assessing look. "Are you all right?"

I nod, swallowing. "Just...brought back some bad memories."

"I won't let anyone harm you," he reassures me. "You're safe."

Nodding again, I hand him the casserole when he puts his hands out, and manage a smile. I'm moving forward, I remind myself. The past is past. That man just wants to get to his job, and I just want to see my friend's—boyfriend's?—apartment. He's not the same man that bought me from the slave houses... and even if he was, I'm better at standing up for myself now. I know what I want and I'm not going to let anyone bully me anymore. I loop my arm in Ainar's, tucking my hand into the crook of his elbow.

All future, no past, I tell myself, and feel better.

Ainar is on the third floor down. He opens the door and gestures that I should go inside first. It's not just politeness—

the apartment itself is very narrow, designed to be functional rather than a space where one would want to spend a great many hours lounging. There's a sitting couch across from a comm panel, a tiny kitchen and lavatory, and in the back adjoining room, a mesakkah-sized bed. The front area is plain other than a local plant growing in a pot, but the back bedroom is fascinating. On one wall, there is an assortment of salvaged screens of all kinds, flipping through vids of exotic locations—a beach here, a jungle there, a grassy meadow elsewhere. At the end of the bed, there's a very large screen and on it, it looks like a view from a farm here on Risda.

Actually, it could be the view from my farm. I point at it, curious. "Did you—"

"It's an old feed," he says quickly. "From before you took over the farm. But yes, it's yours." His tail wags back and forth in a wild arc. "I just...even if you didn't want to see me, I wanted to be close to you."

I smile, because that's rather sweet.

"Before I met you, it was a view from the roof at Port." Ainar gives me a sheepish look. "I like to wake up and see the world outside, and we don't have windows here in the building. But seeing the fields and the settlement, it reminds me how lucky I am to be here and not back home, in an overcrowded neighborhood where my life was all planned out for me. I am grateful."

I completely and utterly understand that. He's moving forward with a healthy appreciation for where he's going, just like me. "Well, if we're talking about things we're grateful for, I'm grateful that your bed is bigger than mine."

His tail starts to thump against his leg. "I am grateful for that, too." He gestures at the casserole in his hands. "Do you wish to eat?"

"I could eat. Show me where your warmer is?"

We head into the tiny kitchen and conversation is easy between us, despite the week apart. I feel as if I've known him forever. We laugh over the same jokes, talk about farming and the weather, and he tells me all about how Sinath had to get an oversized rodent out of a colonist's barn, only for her to want to keep it as a pet.

"You should have seen the look on his face," Ainar tells me between bites of the food. "Here he is, ready to twist the beast's head off and the female is saying 'I shall call him Jerry.'"

I snicker at that, imagining the oversized squirrel-like rodents I've seen in my barn once or twice as a pet named Jerry. "Pets are a big deal back home. I bet she's lonely."

"Poor Sinath didn't know what to do," Ainar continues. "The thing was scratching his arms and he was trying to hold it while she found a cage and—"

There's a thump on the wall behind him. A moan. Another thump. "Harder," a woman's voice says, muffled through the wall. "I said harder!"

"Wow," I manage, choking on my noodles as the bed (at least I think it's a bed?) in the other apartment thumps even faster. "Thin walls, huh?"

Ainar nods, poking at his food with his eating sticks. "My neighbor is a praxiian dock worker. Very polite. Lately he has been dating a..." He struggles for a way to describe her, his face distinctly uncomfortable. "...human woman."

A praxiian and a human? Not the most usual pairing amongst the women I know here on Risda, but there are a few that are married to the cat-like males. "That's sweet."

"It is...something," he agrees, strangled.

Immediately, there's another hard thump on the wall. "Fuck me harder, you brute," the shrill voice demands. "Fuck me like you hate me!"

My eyes go wide. It's *something* all right. "I guess this is a good thing," I murmur to Ainar, leaning over the dinner table. "It's a good reminder that whatever we do, we need to be quiet."

He nods in agreement. "And that I will need to fuck you like I hate you, even if I do not, just so you do not yell at me."

Oh, a silly sense of humor. I really am in danger. "I don't hate you," I say softly. "So I wouldn't ask it."

The look he gives me is smoldering. "Then how would you ask me to fuck you?"

"Like I'm the best thing you've ever seen. Like I'm your entire world and you'll die if you don't get to touch me in the next moment."

"But that is how I always fuck you," Ainar says in a low voice, his gaze locked on my face. "Because it is the truth."

Lord have mercy. My face feels hot—actually, all of me does. "Before we move forward, Ainar, I want to talk about you and me and the baby first." I bite my lip, hoping that we're both on the same page, relationship-wise. It would be hard to turn back right now, but I would if I needed to. "I like you a lot—"

"But you are not certain if you want me to be part of the baby's life?" he finishes. "Because you do not trust me yet after me being a ghost this past week?"

I want to giggle at his phrasing, but this moment feels too momentous. I nod. "I started this with the intention that I'd be the only parent, and just because you and I are getting along right now doesn't mean we will be in six months. You know? So I don't want you with me because you feel like you have to be a parent, and I don't want to feel like I have to stay with you because you're the one that got me pregnant."

Ainar nods. "I understand. This is your child, Naomi. If we are still together when the baby is born—and I intend we shall be—then we will revisit things then. Does that ease your fears?"

It does, actually. It'll allow us to explore being us without the anchor of him being in the child's life. Would I like him to be part of it? Absolutely, but only if we're both still friendly. I've only known Ainar for a week or so and most of that was apart. It's too early for us to decide anything yet, other than that we like each other. "So we're friends that are attracted to each other and made a baby, but that's all."

"You may view us as friends, but in my eyes, you are already more." Ainar's voice is a soft caress. "My people quickly become covetous of their females, and I am already obsessed with you."

"I'll allow it," I joke. It's strange, but I feel safe. I know that even if he's completely infatuated, if I tell him to back off, he will. Heck, he already did. He really is as sweet as he seems.

"Harder!" the voice shrieks from next door.

We both wince.

"Maybe in the future we need to have date nights at my farm," I whisper to him.

Ainar nods. "First thing tomorrow, I am getting you a bigger bed from provisions."

I chuckle at that, because I didn't mind my tiny bed. It allowed us to squeeze in tight next to each other. I get up from my spot at the table and move to his side, brushing my hand up his arm as he gazes at me. "Until then, you're just going to have to be extra quiet, hmm?"

"Me?" Ainar tilts his head back, regarding me. "You whimper every time I thrust into you."

Do I? My entire body clenches with arousal at his words. "Do not."

"You do. Shall I prove it?" His arm encircles my waist as I lean close, and his tail loops around one of my legs. "Shall I put you down on my bed and fill you with my cock and we shall see which one makes more noise?"

"Do it," I dare him. "Because I bet you're not quiet either."

Ainar gets to his feet, looming over me. A year or two ago I would have been utterly terrified of him, his arching horns and muscular build. Of the very alien-ness that stamps his blue features. But now I love them. I love the fact that even though he's oversized, there's a gentleness in his big hands. There's adoration in his eyes when he looks at me, as if I really am the best thing he's ever seen.

He already considers me his. And as he gently picks me up and swings me into his arms, I suspect it won't take long for me to see him as mine, either. I might already be halfway there.

He carries me the short distance to his bed and lays me ever-so-gently atop the blankets. With reverent hands, he pulls my tunic dress off of my body, tugging it over my head and then setting it aside. He does the same with my shoes, and when I'm naked on the bed, he drops to his knees at the side of it and pushes my thighs apart.

"Remember," he breathes. "We must be quiet."

And then he tongues me in the most explicit, obscene way that makes it utterly impossible to remain quiet. He laps at my clit, teasing it with the flat of his tongue, driving me towards a hot, quick climax. I keep expecting him to change things up, to pull back, but he never does. He's not interested in edging me. He's interested in making me come. He's interested in making me scream like a banshee.

When he finds my G-spot deep inside with that thick finger of his, I'm not even the slightest bit ashamed of the wailing noise I make when I climax. When he continues to tongue me, driving me towards another quick, sharp orgasm, I whimper, all right. And when he flips me over and tugs me to my knees, pushing into me from behind with agonizing slowness, making me feel every ridge and piercing exquisitely, I can't even remember what noises I make. Just that I can't stop, and when he starts pounding into me, he's not quiet, either. He grunts with every stroke, making my skin prickle with just how sexy I find it. His spur thumps against my back door with every movement, and instead of irritating me, I find that I start craving that little push against that spot when he bottoms out. And when he puts a hand on the back of my neck, holding me in place while he fucks me?

I'm pretty sure all his neighbors hear.

I'm pretty sure I don't care, either. All I know is that I'm happy.

EPILOGUE

NAOMI

Thirteen Months Later

Getting in and out of the air-sled gets more and more difficult with every month that I'm pregnant. To think that I've still got one or two to go. By the time this baby comes, I'm going to have to be strapped on the hood instead of in one of the seats. Groaning, I turn to the side, pushing the control sticks out of the way as I get to my feet. Once upright, I give my back a moment to adjust, put a hand under the heft of my belly to support it, and waddle toward the custodial office.

"Oh my god, look at how big you are!" a familiar voice squeals when I cross the street. "You get bigger every time I see you." Martina clasps her hands in front of her chest, beaming at me as I make my way. "You're as big as a house."

If I wasn't so big, I think I'd cheerfully murder her for pointing that out. As it is, all I can do is smile politely and pat my belly. It's true. I'm an absolute house. Not just a house. A mansion. A palace. A happy one, though. I rub my belly. "I am definitely growing a full-sized person in here."

"How are things going?" she asks, eyeing my belly with envy. "You and your sweetheart are together every time I see you. You look so great together."

"Ainar is wonderful," I agree. "How are things with you?"

Her expression fades a bit. "Oh, you know. Just living the single life." She brushes a lock of hair back from her face and gazes wistfully at my belly. "What's it like being so pregnant? Miserable?"

"Actually, I kind of love it?" I give my huge belly a pat. "I mean, yeah, my ankles swell up like balloons and my belly is covered in so many stretch marks I look like a zebra, but gosh, it's wonderful. I feel amazing and so connected to this little person."

As if my baby girl is agreeing with me, she gives my belly a kick.

"I'm really happy for you," Martina says, her eyes full of emotion. "You're so lucky you found Ainar just as you were thinking about trying a fertility shot."

"Yup. Isn't that timing incredible?" I say. She doesn't know the truth of how the two of us met. She definitely doesn't need to know that I met Ainar when I showed up at the port office, begging for someone to impregnate me. As far as she knows, it was just the right place at the right time. "So crazy how the universe just threw him in my path."

Martina eyes me with interest. "So what brings you into town this morning? Running errands?"

"Pie," I admit. "I came in for pie. Lucy promised to send one in to the office with Rektar and I can't stop thinking about it." Have I put on weight this pregnancy? Far too much. Do I care? Not in the slightest. Ainar loves my spreading thighs and my huge belly, and if he's happy with them, I'm happy with them too.

I love being pregnant. Love everything about it. The food cravings, the changes in my body, all of it. Most of all, I love the connection with the baby growing in my stomach. I've been lucky in that it's been a breeze. I know people that have been sick for the entire pregnancy or had health problems, but it's been easy for me, as if the universe is finally throwing me a bone.

We chat for a few more minutes about nothing at all. Martina looks good despite her broken heart. Her praxiian boyfriend came back only to rob her of her credits and then took off again. Now she's got no baby, no boyfriend, and no savings. But she keeps her chin up, because if there's one common element of Risda women, it's that we're survivors. We take the shit the universe dishes out at us and we keep on going. Martina will be just fine. We make a lunch date for next week, and then I head into the Port Custodial Office to say hello to my boyfriend and get myself some pie.

The moment I step through the door, I see all of the consulting tables at the front office are busy. Rektar is talking with a pair of newcomers and showing them vids of a sample farm. Sinath is writing notes on his data pad as Lettie complains about the slow response time of her farm bots. Paxon walks out with another woman, strapping on a protective plas helmet that I've seen the men use for insect infestations.

And at another table in the corner, my sweet Ainar sits with his shoulders hunched and a slim tool in his hand, his eyes narrowed in concentration as he works on repairing a data pad for a weepy-looking Christine, who probably dropped hers again. (Ainar tells me she's broken all the equipment at her farm at least once. She's a bit accident prone.)

He looks like he's busy, so I head past the tables, giving Sinath and Rektar a little wave as I do, and head for the back of the office. The men's desks are lined up in neat rows back here, and in the small kitchen of the office, I can see Khex shoving a piece of pie into his mouth.

"I hope you saved some for me," I declare as I head toward him.

Khex's eyes widen as I approach. He swallows quickly and puts a hand to his mouth to shield it from spraying crumbs. "Kef me, Naomi, you're huge!"

I mock-scowl, but I'm kind of used to that reaction. My belly's become increasingly prominent the last few weeks, which I hope is a sign that I'm going to deliver soon, and I've taken to wearing a couple of caftan-like tunics that flow to my ankles but don't exactly slenderize a gal. "I'm going to tell your woman you were being mean to me. Now give me some pie."

He chuckles, a pleased expression on his face as he dishes a large slice of the pie out for me. It's a local root that Lucy manages to make taste like sweet potato, and it makes an amazing pie. He hands me a small plate and I immediately dig in, biting back a moan the moment the heavenly flavor touches my tongue. "Didn't mean it as rude," Khex says. "I was just surprised. You're so tiny and your belly has gotten so big."

"Have you seen Ainar?" I ask between bites. "He's not exactly a tiny guy himself. Of course his baby's big. How's Ashley?"

"Cranky as ever," he says, and the way he says it makes it sound endearing, as if he's delighted in his mate's attitude. "She's coming by later today to celebrate."

"Celebrate what?" I ask, shoving another huge bite of pie into my mouth. Would it be rude for me to eat a second piece, I wonder. Nah. I'll play the pregnant lady card.

"Oh, uh..." Khex wipes his mouth and straightens. "No

reason. Look at the time. I have to head out. See you soon, Naomi." He pats my shoulder and then all but races out of the kitchen, and I frown at his back as he leaves. I'll have to ask Ainar what the deal is.

He can't keep a secret from me. I'm too good at working it out of him.

Smiling to myself, I polish off another piece of Lucy's incredible pie while I imagine the delicious torture I'm going to inflict on my big sexy alien. Tickling, I decide. Definitely tickling. And maybe a blowjob or two. My belly seems to be growing daily, and my libido has skyrocketed as well. It takes everything I have not to pounce on Ainar whenever we're alone.

Heck, maybe I won't even wait until we're alone. I'll just pull him into the nearest supply closet and pretend like we're being quiet. Am I a bit of an exhibitionist when it comes to him? Absolutely. Do I love making him lose his mind when I touch him? Without a doubt.

I'm contemplating all the ways to jump my guy when he heads into the back, looking around. His eyes light up the moment he sees me, and I give him a little wave. "You think anyone would care if I had a third piece of pie?"

A wide smile creases his face. "Save some room. I asked Lucy to make you those sweet and salty buns you like so much."

My jaw drops. My mouth waters. "Oh my god. You did?"

"I did." He pulls out a large food container from under his desk and holds it out to me.

With a squeal, I race toward him as fast as a pregnant lady can move when there's her favorite treat being offered. It isn't that fast, but it feels fast to me. I clutch the box to my chest and the aroma of fresh baked goods hits me. Gazing up at Ainar adoringly, I wonder if any woman was ever as lucky as me. "Have I ever told you that you're amazing?"

He beams at me. "Open it."

"I mean it, Ainar. I wake up every day and I feel lucky to have you." I'm getting all weepy at the thought, because truly, I've lucked out with this man. Just this morning he made me pancakes and did the morning rounds before dawn so I wouldn't have to waddle out there. For me, Ainar is wonderful in all ways. He's great in bed, he listens to me, and we have great conversations. We're on the same page with what we want out of life. If that was all he had to offer, I'd consider myself lucky. But for me, it's the small gestures that make my heart swell. It's me complaining that the air-sled's seat hurts my back and I go out the next morning to find that the padding on the seat has been reinforced. It's me mentioning I love the scent of a particular flower and finding a dozen of them in the house a week later. It's Ainar fixing dinner without me asking, or him going by the tiny library of "human books" in town to see if there's a new one for me.

He's constantly showing me that he's thinking of me and trying to make my life amazing. Which is a pretty tall feat considering that it's already amazing with him in it and a baby on the way, and yet every day I feel more grateful for him than I thought possible.

In the thirteen months I've been pregnant and we've been together, he's never once pressured me about a future for us and the baby. Most girls might worry that it means he's not intending to stay, but I know Ainar. He's giving me the space to make the decisions. He's content to let me lead on this, because he trusts me.

Of course, if he asked, I'd say yes. But I also like that he hasn't asked, because it's just another small way he shows that he trusts me.

And now this. He really is the most amazing man. "Ainar," I breathe, beside myself with emotion. "You really are the most thoughtful—"

"Open it," he nudges again, smiling at me.

"Oh, I'm going to demolish these, have no fear," I tell him, the side of the box pressed against my belly. "But have I told you today how much I love you? How happy you make me? How safe I feel when you're around? I didn't think I needed a guy in my life for that, but when you're with me, I just feel like everything's going to be fine. That even if we don't have the answers, we'll figure it out together. That I'm not alone in any of this. That—"

"Naomi," Ainar says in that patient way of his, tail moving back and forth behind him like a pendulum on steroids. "Please quit telling me how much you like me and just open the box."

Oh. I eye him and the nervous, eager look on his face. The smile that's beaming wide. Oh. I know what this is. Before I even pull the lid off the box, I know there's going to be a ring there. Sure enough, nestled amongst the sticky honey glaze and salt crystals atop the buns, there's a simple, plain metal band, sized for a human finger. Or at least, a human finger that's not puffy with pregnancy. "Oh *Ainar*."

He gets down on his knee, and I want to swoon.

"You've been talking to Lucy, haven't you?" I ask him as he takes the treats box out of my arms and sets it back down on the desk.

He takes my hand in his, rubbing my knuckles. "I have. And she said this is the proper way to do such things. I wish to mate you, my Naomi. To mate, to marry, and to raise our family together. You are my sunrise and my sunset. I am the Rodeo to your Juliet."

"Romeo," I murmur. He's definitely been talking to Lucy.

"But yes, you are."

"I know you wished to remain in control of the situation," he tells me. "And I want you to know that you are yet in control. Even if you cannot accept this ring yet, I wish to give it to you so you know that I am ready, and I am content to wait for the day that you are."

"Even if it takes ten years?" I ask, knowing my answer already.

"Even if it takes fifty," he tells me solemnly. "I am content to remain at your side as your boyfriend, so long as you want me."

Tears prick my eyes. That's one of the things I love most about Ainar. He's content to give without asking for anything back. He just wants those that he loves to be happy, and nothing more is required. He's the most selflessly sweet man I've ever met, human or alien.

So I take the sticky ring from him and slip it on my finger. "What if I'm ready now?"

His grin could put the sun to shame with its brightness. "Then I would take you to City Hall and ask for them to marry us in the human fashion today."

"Can it wait until I have one of those buns?" I lick the honey from my ring and want to moan with how good it tastes. "Actually, can it wait at least an hour?"

Ainar gets to his feet, cupping my face in his big hands. "Of course, my love. What happens in an hour?"

I lick my fingers again, this time with lascivious intent. "An hour should give me enough time to have my way with you in the supply closet."

His tail smacks against the desk with a resounding series of thuds. "I think I would like that," he tells me in a hoarse voice. "I would like that a lot."

So will I.

AUTHOR'S NOTE

Hello there!

This idea was pretty short and sweet. I wanted to write a story with a nice guy and a nice girl and they make a baby. That's about it, really. ;) The nice thing about being an author is that I can have an idea for a scene (the desk one in this book) and just make a whole book around it. Authoring's a fun job, not gonna lie.

I suppose this particular idea came from "What if you got the fertility shot from the doctor on Risda and you missed your window?" I had this mental image of Naomi being this really capable person. She's doing great with her farm, she's got her shit handled, but she needs a man to make a baby with her. She doesn't need a man. Just his jizz.

I liked the idea of turning the tables on the guy and her just needing him for his dick and not wanting a relationship...until she does.

(This *is* a romance, of course.)

But yeah, this is just a guilty pleasure read/write. I think it stemmed from reading a thread online about someone being sick of baby books...so I wrote one. Because I'm not sick of them! I'm sorry! Never let the world yuck your yum!! For those of you not wanting babies in your books, I'll write a non-baby one soon.

If you're wondering about Paxon and Sinath, I'm sure they will eventually get books. Maybe that rogue praxiian that never got Martina pregnant gets one too. Maybe. The universe is wide open!

I hope you enjoy!

— Ruby

WANT MORE?

Of course you do. This is a cute story but it's an *amuse-bouche*. A taste to whet your appetite, so to speak. Lucky for you I have an entire backlist in Kindle Unlimited! Take your pick!

Want more Risdaverse?
When She's Ready
When She Purrs
Risdaverse Tales

Maybe some Corsairs?
The Corsair's Captive
In the Corsair's Bed

Another sweet and fluffy (and slightly horny) stand-alone read?
The King's Spinster Bride
The Half-Orc's Maiden Bride

Enjoy!